T164s

The Sacred Circle of the Hula Hoop

The Sacred Circle of the Hula Hoop

Kathy Kennedy Tapp

Margaret K. McElderry Books
New York

Margaret K. McElderry Books
Macmillan Publishing Company
866 Third Avenue
New York, NY 10022
Collier Macmillan Canada, Inc.

Printed in United States of America

First Edition

10 9 8 7 6 5 4 3 2 1

Library of Congress Cataloging-in-Publication Data

Tapp, Kathy Kennedy.
The sacred circle of the hula hoop.
Summary: In the early 1960s, thirteen-year-old Robin tries, in a variety of ways, to unravel the mystery behind her older sister's dramatic change of personality and attempted suicide.
[1. Sisters–Fiction.   2. Child molesting–Fiction.   3. Suicide–Fiction.
4. Emotional problems–Fiction]
I. Title.
PZ7.T1646Sac   1989   [Fic]   88–27369
ISBN 0–689–50461–6

*Dedicated to the memory of my sister Pat
and to all those whose child within
has been hurt.*

DEEPEST THANKS TO TERRY, FOR THE DREAM
TO BOB, FOR THE CANDLE,
AND TO MY FAMILY AND FRIENDS,
FOR LOVING SUPPORT.

Contents

In a circle
a return is made
to the beginning

———————————

Part 1

Four Days
Before Christmas — 1960

I

I WAS EATING A TUNA-FISH SANDWICH IN THE
kitchen when the gun went off in the bedroom.

From now on, whenever I look at tuna, or even smell
it, my brain will think *bang!* I'll remember . . . running
down the hall to the bedroom . . . finding Jen . . . the red
circle spreading over her pink blouse . . . the gun . . . in
her hand—

No! I slam my mind shut like a door. I cannot bear to
think about this. I *cannot.* I'm getting shaky again. Have to
do something till Mom and Dad get back from the hospital.

They both had to go this time. "We'll be back in an hour
or two, Robin," they told me. "Mrs. Higgins is right next
door. She said she'd check in on you." They said it over and
over.

I don't need Mrs. Higgins. I need something . . . don't
know what. I grab another Christmas cookie. There must
have been three or four dozen cookies on that plate yesterday when it happened. Every time I pass the kitchen counter
now I grab one and stuff it in. Something inside me says:
"This cookie will make me feel better." It only makes my

tongue feel coated in greasy sugar. I thought the last three were going to come back up.

I'm acting so *stupid*. Like when the police asked me, "Robin, how many shots?" I couldn't remember. Now, that's dumb. A thirteen-year-old should be able to count the bangs. But I just sat there and shook my head, and said, "I don't know. I don't remember."

It's embarrassing to think about. Well, I'm not going to sit around here and think about it anymore. I'll walk to the hospital. It's over a mile, but that's okay.

I start out the door. The cold air hits me.

Forgot my coat. I head back to the closet and stop halfway there. What did I come back for?

I grab another cookie. Coat—that was it.

I keep doing such stupid things! Because there is a big, solid icicle in my brain, cold and hard, blocking all my thoughts.

I'll make it all the way out the door this time.

Forgot to change shoes. For crossing the muddy park. But I'm not stopping again. I'm getting out of this house with its cookies and its idiotic, twinkling Christmas-tree lights.

The quickest way is to cut through the backyard, then over through the park. Our backyard is small: a few fruit trees, some honeysuckle, an oleander bush. There's a weedy place between the garage and the fence. There's a rusty old lawn mower and . . . the Hula Hoop. I stop and stare at it.

It's still yellow, but not so bright as it used to be. It has a little dent in the plastic.

Yellow, friendly. Like an old, tired smile in the brown winter grass. A remember-me? kind of smile.

It does what the cookies couldn't do. It starts to break up the icicle inside me. I go over and pick up the Hula Hoop, grasping the cold, hard plastic. I need it. Like a teddy bear. I need its friendliness. I start rolling it along with me, across the street, to the park. It's damp out and cold. My tennis shoes are getting soggy from the grass. My hands are getting wet from the Hula Hoop.

When you stare at things hard enough, something happens to your eyeballs. Everything else sort of fades back, and that one thing becomes bigger, bigger, till it's the only thing in the whole world.

It's that way with the Hula Hoop. I keep looking at it. It had such power—once. It must still have power.

I wish it were magic, like a time machine. I wish I could take it and roll time backward: one circle back to the year I was twelve. Another circle back to the year I was eleven. That's when it all started. With the Hula Hoop. And miracles. That's the year I first knew things were not right with Jen.

Part 2
Sixth Grade

2

"COME ON, ROBIN! KEEP GOING. YOU CAN DO it!" Georgie and Lynn yelled, jumping up and down on the sidelines. "Keep twirling it!" Georgie and Lynn were my best friends in sixth grade.

I didn't answer them, just kept moving and wiggling, swirling the Hula Hoop around my waist, around and around, faster and faster. I'd been doing it for an hour and forty-five minutes. The whole parking lot behind Krueger's store had been filled with all colors of Hula Hoops and all ages of kids when the contest started. Now there were just me and a tall, skinny kid with a purple Hula Hoop. Until a few minutes ago, there'd been a little freckled girl, too. But when the announcer told us to whirl the Hula Hoops up to our necks, she was just too tired. She lost the rhythm, and her hoop fell.

"Knees!" yelled the announcer.

I groaned. Oh boy, that's the hardest, when you're this tired, to slide the Hula Hoop down to knee level without letting it stop whirling, without letting it fall. It's tricky enough when you're fresh and not half dizzy. I started sliding it down, slowly, carefully, over the hips, down to the thighs, then to knee level, twirling it madly so it wouldn't drop the rest of the way to the ground. I didn't want to even *think* about having to get enough speed to work it back up to waist level again.

"Great job!" yelled Georgie.

"Keep it up!" shouted Lynn.

I quickly glanced sideways at the tall, skinny kid. He'd managed to get his hoop to his knees, too. He looked the way I felt. There'd be yellow and purple circles in both our dreams tonight, for sure. And would we be sore—waist, thighs, everything.

"Neck!" yelled the announcer. I stared at him in disbelief. He was grinning. *Grinning.* The monster. Did he really think that at this stage of the game we could work the Hula Hoop all the way back up to neck level without breaking rhythm? He wanted to get the contest over with. That was it.

"Come on, Robin!" Georgie cried.

"Don't give up now!" Lynn must have read my mind. Or maybe she could see my hoop start to wobble just a bit.

"The other kid's slowing down!" Georgie hissed. "You've almost got it!"

I took a deep breath and started my knees going in circular rhythm, faster, faster, to make the Hula Hoop spin faster still; then bending my knees lightly, I forced the hoop up, to thigh level, waist level. I felt dizzy.

"Neck!" the announcer yelled again. It sounded like a warning this time. Get it up there or drop out. I glared at him.

Okay, wise guy. I took another deep breath, then started my whole body circling, not just my waist, letting the hoop gather speed. Tilting sideways, I thrust one arm inside the circle. One-two-*three*. Swing it up, all the way to the neck. Other arm in. And the Hula Hoop was spinning around my neck like a satellite.

I heard noises from the sidelines. A big cry, then Georgie's voice, excited, happy. "He dropped it! You won, Robin!"

I stopped twirling. The Hula Hoop fell. But everything else kept going in circles. My body still felt as though it were spinning. The ground seemed to tilt back and forth. The announcer swayed as he came toward me, holding out a ten-dollar bill.

"First-place prize in the Hula Hoop contest—for keeping the Hula Hoop spinning nonstop for one hour and fifty-five minutes: number twenty-six, Robin McCord!"

3

"WE'RE RICH! WE'RE RICH! NOW WE CAN really have enough money to start our club!" Georgie was dancing around me, smiling, chattering. "I knew you could do it, Robin!"

"That was a great idea we had!" Lynn took the Hula Hoop and started twirling it around her arm.

Our "great idea" had been to put all our nickels and dimes together so we could come up with the one-dollar entry fee for the Hula Hoop contest. We didn't have enough money for all of us to enter. So we'd picked straws to see who'd be the one to do it. I hadn't been Hula-Hooping just for me; I'd been doing it for all of us. And—I stared in amazement at the crisp ten-dollar bill in my hand—I'd actually won the contest! All those other kids who'd dropped out earlier and then stood around and watched—they were all staring at *me,* as if I were some sort of celebrity! And I was. I was the winner! One hour and fifty-five minutes. Except for being dizzy, pooped, and twirled out, I felt great!

"Come on, let's go to the club-spot to celebrate!" Georgie threw her arm around my shoulder and started hauling me off the parking lot and onto the sidewalk. Lynn skipped along beside, still twirling the hoop on her arm.

"To the club-spot!"

"But Robin's got to get to school," Lynn reminded Georgie.

I stopped. I'd forgotten about that. For two hours all I'd thought about was Hula-Hooping. And for the last few minutes, I'd been just standing around, grinning and feeling floaty-happy and floaty-dizzy. I turned to Lynn, worried.

"Did you write me the note?"

"Yep." She patted her pocket. "I took a long time with it, to make it match your mom's writing in the other note you showed me. But I only wrote that you were sick this morning." She looked at her watch. "So you'd better get back after lunch."

"Great." It wasn't fair. Catholic schools always had different spring breaks from the public schools. And the exciting stuff always happened the week the publics were off and the Catholics were slaving away. Like this Hula Hoop contest.

A little shiver of worry broke through the floaty happiness. If Sister Monica found out . . . Oh boy.

I walked faster. I wouldn't think about Sister Monica right now. It was worth it, to be in the contest, to win ten bucks. "I've got time," I said, trying to sound very unconcerned.

"Do I hear what I think I hear?" Georgie pointed down the street cheerfully. The Helmes Bakery van was chiming its way down the block.

Doughnuts! Suddenly I realized how much energy two hours of Hula-Hooping took. Suddenly I realized I was starving.

We all started running toward the bakery van, waving our arms to flag it down; waiting while the driver went to the back of his van and pulled out the long, long drawer that held all kinds of fantastic fresh doughnuts. I just stood there and felt my overworked knees start to go limp and the saliva practically drool out of my mouth. I could almost taste the glaze.

"I'll have one of the glazed and one jelly and one sugar and . . ."

"Hey, Robin, we're not going to spend the whole ten dollars on doughnuts!"

"They're only five cents each. Come on, we can eat them at the club-spot." I grabbed the bag in one hand and the change in the other and took off for my house, half a block away.

Five minutes later we were sprawled in the weeds of the club-spot, stuffing in doughnuts and soaking up sun.

Our club-spot wasn't a real clubhouse, just a little left-over yard between the back of the garage and the fence. It was about six feet wide and ten feet long, and full of weeds except in the part where we'd laid some old boards. Right now the money was on the boards.

"More than nine fifty left," I mumbled, licking glaze off my fingers. "We are rich!"

"Absolutely," Georgie agreed.

The prize money was one of the best things that ever

happened to us. And all because of the Hula Hoop. Our good luck piece. After all, I wasn't so great at Hula-Hooping. Not any better than anybody else. So it must have been the hoop. It brought good luck.

It felt fantastic to just lie in the weeds and munch doughnuts. It felt great to be with Georgie and Lynn, and to see that money lying on our boards. Our club treasury. I was lucky to have such good friends. They'd put their money in with mine for the entry fee. They'd rooted for me. We did *everything* together. Except one thing—school. I was Catholic and they were public. Lynn and Georgie didn't have any religious education. I learned catechism and I knew all about saints and God and Mass and everything. But they didn't know any of it. So I sometimes taught them. I taught them catechism and I read them the good parts in the saints books: the ones who died for their faith and were boiled in oil or beheaded. I even baptized Georgie. I figured that made her an honorary Catholic. Lynn was already baptized.

So now we finally had money for a real club. With a treasury.

"Isn't this the best day ever?" I said.

"Right," agreed Georgie.

"We're best friends."

"And this is *our* club-spot. Just for us."

"Right," Georgie said again.

"We should have a friendship ring," Lynn said thoughtfully.

"What?"

"A friendship ring. I read about them in a book. Really good friends have them."

Lynn read a lot of books. If she said we needed a friendship ring, she knew what she was talking about.

"Hey, what about *that* for a friendship ring?" I pointed to the Hula Hoop. "It's a big ring! And it's lucky."

"Not that kind of ring. You have to be able to put it on."

"We could put that on!" I jumped up. "I'll show you." I grabbed the yellow Hula Hoop and set it on the ground. "Okay, step in," I commanded. "And keep your arms down."

When they were standing inside the hoop, I reached down and lifted it up, till it was around all three of us, like a hard belt, squeezing us into a tight circle.

"We are now in the friendship ring," I said solemnly, sucking in my stomach and tilting my head back so I didn't knock it against Georgie's.

"And we will forever be friends," added Lynn, catching on to the ceremony.

"Amen," said Georgie, shutting her eyes tightly, as though she were praying.

"Amen." I dropped the hoop to the ground. Then I noticed my watch.

"Oh, my gosh!" Lunch recess would be almost over. "I'll never make it back to school in time! Bye!"

I raced into my house, wiped off the doughnut crumbs, changed into my brown-and-yellow uniform, and flew out the door.

"Please, God, don't let lunch recess be over," I prayed, running down the street so fast my stomach cramped. "Please, God, don't let Sister Monica know that my mom didn't write that note!"

4

GOD ANSWERED MY PRAYER. SISTER MONICA wasn't even at school. Sister Agnes Joseph was in charge for the day.

Of all the nuns at St. Ignatius School, Sister Agnes Joseph was the most fierce. She stood as straight as a telephone pole, and when she got angry she seemed to suddenly grow about six inches taller, until she loomed over you, dark and terrible in her crisp black habit and veil. Even the biggest, toughest boys scrunched down at their desks and tried to look invisible when Sister Agnes Joseph went on the warpath.

Sister Agnes Joseph and I didn't get along too well, ever since the first day when she looked at my name on the attendance sheet and said, staring hard at me: "And with all the saints in heaven, why did your parents choose to name you after a bird?"

Usually she had our class only for religion. But I'd prayed, "Don't let Sister Monica guess about my note," so God gave Sister Monica the flu and He sent Sister Agnes Joseph to our class for the whole day. From now on, I'd better word my prayers more carefully.

I handed Sister Agnes Joseph Lynn's note and waited with my heart Ping-Ponging inside my uniform.

But two hours of Hula-Hooping and two doughnuts and a half-mile run to school had all done their work on me. Sister Agnes Joseph looked at me over her glasses.

"Do you feel all right now, Robin?"

I breathed a long, shaky sigh of relief. She believed.

"Yes, Sister," I gulped.

"Then take your seat." She spoke so slowly and distinctly, she almost chewed the words. "We are doing Religion."

I heard a little "psst" from the seat behind me as I slid into my desk. Tommy O'Brien. "God and the devil," he whispered.

"Thanks," I whispered back. Tommy knew how to take Sister's fifteen-thousand-word lecture and sift it down to two.

"Now, class, as I was saying, the devil is very much alive in the world today. He's just waiting for a chance to lead you into sin." Sister stood very tall. She practically touched the ceiling. Her voice was hushed, but even so, it filled every corner of the room. "The devil is very clever. . . ."

I gulped. I could practically see Satan at the window, his red eyes like fireballs, his pitchfork in his hand.

I felt a little jab behind me. "You can always tell if it's the devil," Tommy whispered behind his hand. "My mom told me how. The devil has one foot like a horse. That's how you tell."

"Okay," I whispered back, looking at the floor, at all the feet under the desks.

"But your best weapon against the devil is your faith," Sister went on sternly. "That's the problem with the world today. People have no *faith*. Think of all the miracles that happened in the old days, boys and girls. Blind men seeing, lame men walking, *visions*—" She jabbed her yardstick at us with each word. "In the old days, when people had faith, they saw Jesus, the Blessed Mother, the saints. But now"— she shook her head sadly—"all they care about is material things. *Money!*"

I gulped again. I thought of the prize money on my shelf at home.

"When people are always thinking of money, there is no room for God in their lives." Sister banged the yardstick on the desk. "Jesus said it is easier for a camel to go through the eye of a needle than for a rich man to get into heaven. Think of that, boys and girls." Sister's gaze swept the class. It seemed to me that her eyes stayed a second longer on me. "It is *that* hard to get into heaven if you are always thinking about money."

I sat very still in my seat. I hardly breathed. In my head I saw the ten-dollar bill get bigger and bigger, waving in front of me. Green and Evil.

The prize money was going to keep me out of heaven. That, on top of my ditching school and asking Lynn to forge a note. Oh boy. The sin of it all. I was just one of those people the devil was looking for. On my way home from school, I'd really have to watch people's feet.

5

WHEN I WALKED THROUGH THE FRONT
door of my house, I forgot all about my plans to call
Georgie and Lynn.

Jen was home! She was standing in the kitchen in a
flowery Hawaiian muumuu and opening a package of hot
dogs.

"Robin!" She threw down the hot dogs and grabbed a
big heap of pink tissue-paper flowers from the table. It hung
from her hand in a bright pink circle.

"Happy birthday!" she cried, putting the lei around my
neck. "A wreath of flowers for *you.*" Then she ran out to
the hi-fi in the living room. Soft Hawaiian music started
playing.

I stared at her, wide eyed for a second. Then I started
giggling. "Jen, you're nuts! It's not my birthday!"

"Well, not exactly," she said, heading back into the
kitchen. "Not for two weeks. But Gary asked me to come
and meet his parents on the week that's *really* your birthday.
Gary and I have been seeing a *lot* of each other. This may
get serious. So, anyway"—she waved her arm around the
kitchen, with its tissue-paper flowers hanging from lights,

the music, her muumuu, my lei—"I came today to celebrate early! Happy birthday!" She laughed.

Her muumuu was pink and yellow, with big lavender flowers printed across it. She was wearing sandals and her blond hair was fluffed around her face. Her eyes looked sort of lavender, too. Probably eye shadow.

Jen was even more beautiful in Hawaiian dress than in her usual skirts and sweaters.

"It's going to be a luau party," Jen declared, going back to the hot dogs. "Only of course I couldn't afford a pig like people roast for *real* luaus, so it'll be 'Hot Dogs Hawaiian.' If I can ever figure out how to get the little pineapple pieces stuffed inside." She made a small slit in one of the hot dogs and started trying to cram in a slippery pineapple chunk. "Wait'll you see the cake!" she bragged.

"But . . . but . . ." I didn't quite know what to say. It was such a surprise: her appearing like a fairy godsister in the middle of the kitchen, whipping up a party, instead of being at UCLA taking her art classes. What a day. That yellow Hula Hoop was definitely the luckiest thing I had ever gotten my hands on. First the contest money and now *this.*

"These are going to be the most terrific hot dogs you've ever tasted," Jen assured me, pushing in more pineapple. "I made a sweet-and-sour sauce to go on top. That's the way to do things—classy, Robin." She shook her hair back, away from her face. "If hot dogs are all you can afford, then make 'em the classiest hot dogs in town. Hot Dogs Hawaiian!"

Classy. That was Jen, top to toe. If she hadn't wanted to study art, she could have become a famous movie star, probably.

She'd rather have one stylish outfit from a fancy, expensive shop than ten dresses from a regular, cheap store. And then she'd figure out ten different ways to dress it up, to make it look like a whole bunch of outfits.

"Done." She shoved the hot dogs aside. "Come here, Robin. If we undo your braid, your hair will be so wavy and long. . . ." She started pulling off the rubber band. "Now if Mom were here, she'd say—"

"Don't brush hair in the kitchen!" I chimed in with her, laughing. She ran her fingers through the braided strands, fluffing them apart.

"Now, we'll put a little tissue flower in front, like so. . . ." She stepped back to study her work. I felt strange, with the tissue flower and the lei and my hair falling in kinky waves all over my shoulders. With that music going, I felt almost like a Hawaiian princess.

"Terrific!" Jen smiled. "Mom and Dad'll be so surprised!"

Mom and Dad *were* surprised.

"Jen!" Mom cried when she came home from work. "I thought this was exam week!" Then her eyes went to the muumuu, the lei, the decorations. "What in the world . . ."?

"But it isn't Robin's birthday yet," Dad said when Jen tried to explain to him. He looked completely baffled. "We haven't even had Easter!"

"Robin doesn't mind celebrating, do you?" Jen set the platter on the table. "Dig in, everyone!"

The hot dogs were great, even if the pineapple did slide out. The coconut cake was great, complete with twelve candles. The tropical sherbet was great, too.

"And now for the present." Jen handed me a big flat box with a pink tissue flower on top. "Not quite Hawaiian." She laughed. "Not even a real present. Just something I did in art class."

"You're giving me one of your paintings?" I squealed, pulling off the ribbon. I'd been asking her to paint me something for ages. Jen did some really neat things. I especially liked the merry-go-round she'd painted last year. Maybe that's what was in the box. I yanked back the lid and peeked in.

A little girl's face stared back at me from a wooden frame. A little girl with long hair falling over her shoulders, and a sad, wistful, faraway look on her face.

It wasn't the sort of picture I'd had in mind at all. Not anything like the colorful, cheery merry-go-round.

"Thanks, Jen." I tried to sound enthusiastic. "It's cute. I'll hang it in my bedroom."

Mom stared at the picture over my shoulder. She looked at it for a long time. "The little girl looks so sad," she said finally.

"Well, that's true art. To capture a mood, a moment," Jen said, looking pleased. She came over to study it, too. "I like that picture," she said thoughtfully. "I'm satisfied with it." Then she patted me on the shoulder. "Anyway, it's just for now. I'll bring you a real present next time I come." She yanked me out of my chair. "Out, out, Robin. You are *not* to help clean up. It's your birthday party." Jen scooted me into the living room. "Go play the piano or something."

I giggled. Suddenly it was very funny. I mean, it wasn't even my birthday. And here I was opening presents, getting out of doing dishes . . . "You're nuts," I said, still giggling. She hulaed back into the kitchen.

I set the picture carefully on the couch. Actually, the more I looked at it, the more I liked it. The little girl was so real-looking, even if she was so sad.

I sat down at the piano and started plunking the keys—one of the songs we'd been learning in choir for Lent. It was real easy to play. Only a few notes over and over. . . .

Suddenly Dad was beside me, shaking his head, his hands covering my fingers on the keys.

"Don't play that," he said in a low voice.

"Huh?" I stared up at him.

"It makes Jen sad," he said. "Play something else, okay, Robin?"

"Sure," I whispered back, confused. He patted me on the shoulder and left.

It was just a simple little Lenten song:

At the cross her station keeping
Stood the mournful mother weeping.
Close to Jesus to the last.

Wow. I'd never really thought about the words before.

We just blared them out in choir. It *was* sad. But then, the songs for Lent were supposed to make you feel sad, weren't they? Because of Jesus dying and all?

"Mom, I brought my suitcase." It was Jen's voice, from the hall. "I'm staying over. Okay?"

"But what about your classes?"

"I'm done with my exams. I want to stay over."

"Jen." Mom's voice was low, concerned. "Are you . . . okay?"

"I'll be better if I stay *here* tonight."

The phone rang. It was Georgie.

"Robin, I just got the *best* idea for how to spend some of the prize money! I was talking to Bobby Johnson . . ."

Jen walked by. "I'll go get my suitcase out of the car, Mom," she called.

"White mice!" Georgie was whispering into the phone. "Isn't that a *great* idea? He'll even sell us the cage to keep them in!"

From where I was standing with the phone, I could see Jen staring across the living room; her face didn't have a luau party look at all. It was more like the kind of look you see when people take a deep breath and get ready to do something they dread.

Was something wrong? "Jen—" I started to say, but then the look was gone, the smile was back.

"I'd better get my suitcase," she said cheerily and hurried out the door.

"What?" cried Georgie into the phone. "What did you say?"

"Never mind. I'll talk to you tomorrow, okay, Georgie?"

I hung up the phone and sat there, picking crumbs out of my lei, staring at the picture of the little girl.

Today was definitely one of the wackiest days of my eleven years.

It was great having Jen stay overnight. Just like old times before she went away to college. Yakking through breakfast, plopping on her bed afterward, trying on her jewelry and makeup while she showered.

"Hey, Jen, can I wear your sweater?" I yelled into the bathroom. We were just about the same size; she was so slim and short.

"Yeah," she shouted over the running water. "But be careful; don't stretch it!"

I pulled it carefully over my head, then stared at myself in the mirror. Not bad. Now I needed lipstick.

Her makeup case was on the floor by the bed. I started rummaging through it. Tangerine, strawberry ice, mauve . . . This was fun!

"Robin, quit fooling around," Mom called. "You have school today, remember?"

"Okay." I dropped the stuff back in. There was a notebook by the cosmetics case, shoved partway under the bed. Jen had doodled all over the purple cover. I picked it up. Was it more sketches?

There were no pictures inside, just some writing. Reports, maybe? I started to shut it; then my eye caught the first sentence.

The little girl again. Trapped in a cave.

Was it a story? I read on.

Dark in the cave. And cold. Trying to get out. Feeling terror, panic. The ledge is cold and slippery. There's light ahead. Running. Running toward the light. See something move on a ledge.

A snake.

No way to get out. Trapped.

The words brought goose bumps to my arm. I shouldn't be reading this without asking Jen. That was prying. But I couldn't stop my eyes from going down to the next paragraph.

I'm walking through a forest. But instead of trees, there are giant alphabet letters all around me. The letters are very friendly. Every now and then I dance with a letter. I am trying to make words with the giant letters. I keep walking through the forest to find the word I want. But I can't find it.

Wow, what a strange idea for a story—a forest of giant letters. Maybe Jen was writing a little kids' picture book. It would be fun to see pictures of a kid walking through a forest of giant letters. And maybe it wasn't so strange that Jen would dream about letters. I remember when I was real little she used to come home from school all the time with ribbons she won in spelling bees. The ribbons were still in her scrapbook. She was really good at spelling. And she always beat everyone in Scrabble. Gary, her boyfriend, teased her about spending her spare time reading the dictionary.

The shower water wasn't running anymore. Jen could come out any minute.

I shut the notebook and set it back down on the floor exactly where I'd found it. Then I grabbed a lipstick and sat there innocently twirling it in my fingers, while my eyes kept going back to the notebook.

Were they stories? Then why weren't they finished?

"*Robin!*" Mom yelled for the second time. "You're going to be late for school!"

"Get a move on, lazy." Jen grinned, walking out of the bathroom with a towel wrapped around her head like a turban. "And you're not old enough for lipstick yet. Next year, maybe. Light pink."

I opened my mouth to ask about the notebook, then shut it. I shouldn't have been snooping. She'd be mad.

I tossed her the lipstick. "See ya later, alligator." And I breezed out the door.

But all the way to school I just kept thinking about everything: the stories, the little girl trapped in a cave, the forest of giant letters. Weird. That look last night on Jen's face; Dad telling me not to play that song and Mom asking Jen, "Are you all right?"

A little tiny knot in my stomach said things were not all right.

But . . . *what* was wrong?

6

MY BOOK REPORT! WITH JEN AND THE LUAU
and all, I forgot all about the book report until I walked
into the classroom the next morning and saw Sister Agnes
Joseph standing straight and tall by the blackboard. So Sister
Monica was still sick and Sister Agnes Joseph was still
substituting. Maybe Sister Agnes Joseph didn't even know
that book reports were due.

I couldn't take any chances. Having Sister Agnes Joseph
mad at you was worse than going under the wheels of a
moving train. She didn't use that yardstick only as a pointer.

Slowly, carefully, I propped my book-report book in
front of me and opened my catechism book behind it so
Sister couldn't see. Too bad I hadn't picked a skinnier book.
But the boys always grabbed all the skinny books from the
church library first; those and the ones about the martyrs
who died horrible and bloody deaths. By the time I'd get
there, only the thick books and the boring saints were left.

"Good morning, boys and girls," Sister Agnes Joseph said
slowly, distinctly, as though that was the most important
sentence ever uttered. "Get out your catechisms."

I'd have to keep my head up, as if I were listening to

Sister, and keep my eyes down, reading as fast as eyeballs could go.

Sister Agnes Joseph talked on and on. I got through chapter one. It was about three shepherd children in a place called Fatima, Portugal. The Blessed Virgin Mary appeared to them in a vision and told them they had to do penance and make sacrifices because the world was full of sin. At first no one believed that they'd really had a vision. But after a while, lots of people started coming to Fatima. And then—my eyes almost popped out of my head at the next part—Our Lady made the sun *dance*. Right up there in the sky, in front of thousands of people. I reread the page three times, to make sure it said what I thought it said. Wow. That was the best miracle I'd ever heard of. The sun *dancing*. And for three kids just my age!

"Robin McCord." Sister's voice broke into my thoughts, sharp and stern. I jumped. Everyone was looking at me. Oh, no. A terrible, awful feeling of dread poured through my whole body.

"What was I just saying, Robin?" Sister had that cat-playing-with-a-mouse look. As if she *knew* she had me. My mind raced frantically, trying to remember some of the words that had floated by while I was reading. Faith. Faith. Sister Agnes Joseph usually said the same things over and over half a million times. Maybe she'd kept on the same lesson as yesterday.

I heard a tiny cough behind me. "Sin. God," Tommy whispered and coughed again.

Good old Tommy O'Brien. So it was the same lecture.

"Uh . . ." My voice was shaky, I was so nervous. "Uh . . . you were saying that . . . people think too much about money, and, uh, so . . . we don't have any miracles anymore." Why was she picking on me, anyway? Did she know I had some money?

"Not exactly. You should listen more carefully, miss." Those dark eyes bored right through me. They could probably see through everything but cement.

"Yes, Sister." I gulped. I wasn't off the hook yet. She was probably trying to think of another question, to stump me. "Sister," I said quickly to sidetrack her, "if people did all that penance and sacrifice, would there really still be miracles today?"

"Indeed there would." Sister nodded sternly. "But people today are so busy rushing around, they probably wouldn't even notice."

"But people still go to church." Theresa Williams raised her hand and spoke at the same time.

"That is not enough." Sister lowered her voice. "Do you know what Jesus called people who went to church on Sunday and did all sorts of wicked things during the rest of the week? He called them 'whited sepulchers.' " From the hushed dramatic way Sister said it, it sounded like something *awful*.

"Do you know what that means, boys and girls? A sepulcher is a tomb. A place where they put *dead* people. So a whited sepulcher is a tomb that's painted all nice and pretty white on the outside and"—she made a horrible, disgusted face—"full of rotting *dead* things on the inside.

Maggots. And *that's* what people are like when they pretend to be good."

Uh-oh. I felt something flip-flop in my stomach. Was it a rotting, smelly maggot?

Sepulcher. Tomb. Sin. Maggots. It was awful.

With a sad, sinking feeling, I suddenly knew what I had to do with the Hula Hoop money.

"They're the cutest little mice!" Georgie said, as soon as we met at the club-spot after school. "There are three of them, one for each of us. And I know just where we can keep them—"

"I have an idea, too," Lynn cut in. "We should make this a cooking club. I've been thinking about it all day. See, we buy all the ingredients with the Hula Hoop money and we make something good, like cookies or fudge. Then we sell them and make *more* money!"

They weren't helping at all, either of them. I took a deep breath. "Wait a minute. I have to tell you about something." I opened my book and plopped down on the grass in front of them. "Listen to *this*." I thumbed through, looking for the miracle page. "Here it is. 'In Fatima, Portugal, Our Lady appeared to three shepherd children in a vision and made the sun *dance*.'" I looked up triumphantly. "Isn't that fantastic!"

They looked confused. "Who's our lady?" Georgie asked.

"What's Fatima?" said Lynn. "And what's that book got to do with us?"

I sighed. "Our Lady is Mary. You know—Jesus's mother. And Fatima is some place in Portugal."

"Where's that?"

"I don't know. But it's not in the United States. The people there are shepherds."

"So what's it got to do with us?" Lynn asked impatiently.

"It's got to do with us because . . ." I slammed the book shut. "Because that miracle happened to three kids just like us, almost. So . . . so if *we* do penance and make sacrifices, a miracle could happen to *us*. Right here." I hit the ground with my fist, as if I were Sister Agnes Joseph with her yardstick.

Georgie looked at me suspiciously. "What's penance and sacrifice?"

"Well, it's like . . . giving up things. You know. Stuff like candy and dessert and money—"

"Money!" they cried together.

"Not our Hula Hoop money," Georgie said in a worried voice.

"Well, maybe part of it." I had to talk them into it. I had to get rid of those rotting, smelly maggots.

"I don't want to do sacrifice. I want to buy those cute little white mice. There're three of them and they're so cute—"

"Don't you want to make a miracle happen?" I demanded. "Don't you want to see the sun dance? Help get rid of all the sin in the world?"

"But those little mice are so cute—"

"What about my idea?" Lynn demanded. "If we made

fudge and stuff, we could raise more money and give *that* up," she said reasonably. "How about that, Robin? Would that be a good sacrifice?"

"Wait a minute," said Georgie. "I told Bobby we'd probably buy the mice. And we could keep the cage in the old shed in my backyard. My mom and dad would never find it there."

She was right. Her parents owned a restaurant and they were gone most of the time. They probably never even went into the backyard, much less the old shed.

Little white mice *were* cute and fuzzy. They'd make perfect club mascots. And if they came with their own cage, and we only had to worry about food . . .

"How much does Bobby want for the mice?" I asked, weakening.

"Just a couple of dollars. It's really for the cage. He'd give the mice away. His mom doesn't know the mother mouse had babies. She thought it was a boy."

"Look." Lynn took over, pulling a scrap of paper and a two-inch pencil stub out of her pocket. "We have ten dollars minus the doughnuts, right? So, we buy the mice and some food for a few dollars, and we buy some ingredients to make fudge for a few dollars, and we sell the fudge. Then we'll have lots of money to sacrifice—" She stopped and frowned. "Who are we sacrificing the money *to,* anyway?"

"Oh, church or poor people or something." I waved my hand vaguely. "Doesn't really matter, as long as we don't spend it on ourselves."

"Hey!" Georgie cried. "If we sell the fudge, we'll be

giving *that* up, too. Somebody else will be eating it. That'd be a sacrifice!"

"I . . . guess so." Something didn't sound right about that, but I wasn't sure what.

"How long do you have to do sacrifices before you get a miracle?" Lynn asked, chewing on her pencil.

"I don't know. They didn't teach us that in catechism." I didn't like sounding so unsure. "But I think it'd take a *lot* of sacrifices to make a big miracle like the sun dancing."

"Do you really think"—Georgie tilted her head back to stare at the sky—"do you really think it could happen? The sun dancing?"

"Sister said so. And she knows about things like that. That's what nuns are experts at."

"And we'd be famous." Lynn was sounding more interested now, too.

"Of course. Those kids at Fatima got really famous. Thousands of people came to see them."

"Wow." Georgie leaned back against the fence with a dreamy smile on her face.

"They'd call us the Three Children of California!" Lynn added.

"So we make fudge *and* miracles *and* get the mice." Georgie smiled happily. "I'll go tell Bobby we'll buy them!"

"And we can shop for the cooking stuff on Saturday." Lynn jumped up.

"Don't forget about the sacrifices," I reminded them. "We have to start right away. Even tonight. We should keep a list of what we give up." That idea just popped into my head.

They both nodded solemnly. Lynn grabbed the Hula Hoop from where it was leaning against the fence. "And we should end every meeting with our friendship ring."

"Right." We all stepped into it like before and pulled it up around us like a tight bracelet.

"We will always be friends," we chanted together. I felt saintly, virtuous. No more worry, *and* a white mouse in the bargain!

"Amen!" I said happily.

7

IT WAS HARD TO GET TO SLEEP THAT NIGHT. I kept thinking of our club, the mice we were going to get after school tomorrow, and the great things we'd cook if we figured out whose kitchen we could use. I was also thinking about the piece of cake I'd given up after dinner.

"No thanks," I'd declared as Mom came toward me with a slice of leftover coconut cake. "I don't want dessert to-night." I'd felt so noble, like a real saint. Nothing to this sacrifice business. And I'd written GAVE UP PIECE OF CAKE in my sacrifice notebook.

But later in the evening when I wasn't so full from dinner, I kept thinking about that cake plate and that piece of cake, already cut, sitting there, smothered with coconut cream frosting.

I wanted that cake. Never in my whole life had I wanted anything so much. Even as I lay in bed, I could still see that slice of cake lying on the plate.

My stomach rumbled.

I started to get up. I lay back down.

I could scrape the icing off; give that part up and just eat the cake. That'd still be a good sacrifice.

But the icing was the best part. Maybe I should eat the icing and give up the cake.

But that'd be too sweet.

Maybe I should eat the whole thing and then tear off the first sheet in my notebook. Nobody would ever know what happened.

I got up again.

I was halfway down the hall between my bedroom and the kitchen when the phone rang. I stood stock-still, feeling like a criminal caught in the act, as Mom's footsteps padded across the kitchen floor.

"Hello—" And then her tone changed. "Jen, what's wrong?"

There was a long minute of silence. I stood pressed against the wall. I couldn't decide whether to do the honorable thing and show myself, or just stand there and eavesdrop.

"When you were little?" Mom sounded surprised, upset. "But Jen, I've already told you all I can remember about your childhood. I don't know what else to tell you. Why does he need to know so much about that?"

I heard Dad's loud mutter from the living room: "Fool headshrinkers."

"But Jen—"

Another silence. Then, "All right. I will. I promise. I'll think about it. Yes, yes. Okay, try to get some sleep. Goodbye, honey." She hung up the phone and walked out into the hall—and saw me. "Robin."

No use pretending I wasn't listening. I might as well

barge ahead. "Mom, what's the matter with Jen?"

She sighed. "Jen's having . . . problems."

"What kind of problems?"

"Well," Mom hesitated. "It's hard to explain. I'm not even sure. You see, she gets . . . upset." Mom snapped off the light, then headed us both back to my bedroom. "She's going to a doctor. He'll help her."

"Going to a *doctor,* for being upset?"

"A psychiatrist."

My eyes opened wide. *"Psychiatrist!"*

"Don't say it like it's a dirty word, Robin," she said sternly. "They're qualified doctors, just like Dr. Stearns, our family doctor. And they take care of the kind of troubles that Jen's having. I'm sure this doctor will be able to help her, so you don't have to worry about it, Robin. Jen'll be fine. She knows we all love her." She helped me into bed. "Okay?"

"Yeah. Okay."

It wasn't okay. A psychiatrist. My wonderful big sister going to a psychiatrist. Those doctors were supposed to be for people who weren't . . . right, not somebody like Jen: smart, pretty, artistic, just about perfect.

I thought about Dad standing beside me at the piano, shaking his head and saying, "Don't play that. It makes Jen sad." I thought about the look on Jen's face for that one second the night of my party. Grim, scared.

What was wrong with her?

I got into bed. My stomach didn't even want that cake anymore.

8

"AREN'T THEY THE CUTEST LITTLE THINGS you've seen in your life?" Georgie gushed, cuddling the furry little white balls in her hand. "All three of them *and* the cage, for only four dollars."

I nuzzled my mouse against my cheek. So tiny and so soft. I was really glad that Georgie had talked us into buying them instead of sacrificing all our money. I was glad to be here in the club-spot and thinking about baby mice, instead of thinking about last night, the phone call, Jen.

"What should we call them?" Lynn stroked hers with her fingers. Its little pink nose wiggled.

"How about Fuzzy? Or Whitey?" Georgie said.

"That's what everybody calls white mice." I studied my little mouse thoughtfully. "We should think of something original, to do with our club."

"Well," Lynn said, "we're going to make fudge and miracles, so . . ."

"So let's call them Fudge and Miracle!" I chimed in. "That would be perfect! Yours can be Fudge, Lynn. It's got that little brown spot on its tail."

"But we have three mice," Georgie said. "What should we name mine? Sacrifice?"

"No, but . . . maybe we could name him after a saint," I said slowly. "That would fit."

"Jesus," said Georgie.

I looked at her, shocked. "You can't name a mouse Jesus!"

"You said name him after a saint. That's the only saint's name I know."

I sighed. "Jesus isn't a *saint.* He's the Son of God. And it'd probably be a sin to name a mouse after Him. Don't they teach you anything in public school?"

She glared back. "You think you're so smart, just because you go to Catholic school. We don't need to know all that stuff anyway!"

"Yes you do," I said sternly. "I baptized you, so you're an honorary Catholic. So you do need to know it all."

"All right!" Lynn cut in. "Stop fighting. We won't name your mouse Jesus. Think of another saint, Robin. A saint that wouldn't mind a mouse being named after him."

"That's it!" I yelled, waving my little mouse, Miracle, in the air. "There is a saint like that! He liked all the animals. Even spiders. Saint Francis! We can name your mouse Saint Francis!"

"Okay." Georgie smiled again, happy. "My mouse will be Saint Francis." She petted her little ball of fur. "I hope you're a boy."

"I have to get home early." Lynn got up, holding Fudge carefully. "We better get these guys settled."

"The cage is all ready in the shed," Georgie said. "And Bobby gave me some food, too. But we have to be sure to *always* get them put away before my parents get home—" She looked up as the chimes of the bakery van rang down the street.

"Doughnuts," she said in a completely different voice. Soft, wistful, longing. "Glazed doughnuts. That's just what I need. We still have a lot of money left, Robin."

"We can't. We have to give them up," I said sadly. The chimes were so loud now, the van was probably right in front of my house. I could picture the doughnut drawer all full of luscious things: cookies, brownies, doughnuts. All we needed to do was run out to the curb and flag it down. . . . "We can't," I said again loudly to stop these thoughts of temptation. "It's part of the sacrifice."

"But . . . but . . ." Georgie's voice trailed off. The three of us sat in silence as the chimes grew fainter and fainter.

"Good-bye, doughnuts," Georgie said sadly. She stood up. "This life of penance and sacrifice is hard on a person."

"Well, it'll be worth it to see the sun dance," I said.

"Yeah." Georgie didn't sound convinced.

"Right." Lynn stared off down the street.

"Meeting dismissed," I said in my most noble, suffering voice.

We set down the Hula Hoop, stepped inside its circle, and drew it up around us. "We will always be friends."

"Amen."

Our hoop ceremony was beginning to feel as religious to us as church.

9

THURSDAY. THREE O'CLOCK. THE BEGINNING
of a glorious week of Easter vacation, and also the day of
our first official cooking-club shopping trip.

Lynn brought the cookbook and pencil and paper to the
club-spot. I brought the sacrifice notebook. Georgie
brought Miracle, Fudge, and Saint Francis in a small wicker
sewing basket.

"I just couldn't bear to leave them behind," Georgie
explained, opening the lid and handing them around. "Anyway, it's so dark in that shed. They need their daily sun-
bath."

I set Miracle on my shoulder and brought out my list.
"Okay, what sacrifices did everyone do?"

"I gave up seconds on dinner," Georgie said promptly.

"What did you have for dinner?" asked Lynn suspiciously.

"Uh . . ." Georgie was suddenly very busy petting Saint
Francis's pink nose. "Uh, let me think. Oh yeah, I remember
now. It was split-pea soup."

I wrote GAVE UP SECONDS ON SPLIT-PEA SOUP in the notebook. Sure didn't sound like much of a sacrifice. I looked up.

"Georgie," I said sternly, "do you *like* split-pea soup?"

"Yes," she said in a very definite tone. "It's the best. All that ham and everything." I looked at her suspiciously. Georgie had been known to lie.

"Oh, and I gave up dessert, too. Everyone else in the family had lemon meringue pie, but I said: 'No thanks. I really don't care for any,'" Georgie went on grandly.

"Did you *really*?" Lynn and I were both staring at her now.

"Yes. I *did*."

I wrote down Georgie's second sacrifice and then put a question mark beside it. Georgie had been known to lie a *lot*.

"I gave up extra-credit problems for homework," Lynn announced. I opened my mouth, but she rushed ahead before I could protest.

"I really wanted the extra credit, too. If I'd done the extra credit, I'd probably have gotten an A in math." She sighed loudly. "Those problems were important. It was a hard sacrifice."

"I gave up a piece of coconut cake," I announced. I was really glad now that I hadn't licked the icing off. It would have been embarrassing to have to tell Georgie and Lynn that I'd given up a piece of cake after I'd eaten all the icing.

"Anything else?" I looked around. "Well, then . . ." I shut the notebook and reached back with my other hand to grab Miracle from inside my blouse, where he was climbing around.

"I brought you a book, Georgie. I held it up. It's about your mouse's patron saint, Saint Francis."

"Really?" Georgie sat up. "*My* Saint Francis?" As if he were her own personal saint just because her mouse was named after him. "What did he do?"

"He did a lot." I'd read some of the book before I checked it out from the church library. "I bet he did more sacrifices than any other saint that ever lived! Here, just look at this page."

Lynn grabbed the book and started reading. Georgie sat there smugly, as if she could take personal credit for all of Saint Francis's good deeds.

"Wow!" Lynn breathed. "Oh, yuck. Saint Francis ate garbage out of other people's garbage cans. And he put ashes on his head. And he wore a hair shirt!" She looked up, wide eyed. "Did they really make shirts out of hair back then?"

"Just saints did," I explained. "They itched and scratched. It was part of the penance and sacrifice. The ashes, too."

Georgie stared at my braid, then at Lynn's smooth, long, dark hair. "I don't think our hair would itch and scratch," she said thoughtfully. "They probably didn't have very good shampoos and cream rinses back then." She looked at her mouse and giggled. "My Saint Francis has a hair shirt, too!"

Lynn shut the book. "Enough about him. Let's get the cooking stuff! I already looked up fudge recipes. We just need sugar and unsweetened chocolate and corn syrup . . . hey, Fudge!" She grabbed her mouse from where he was crawling around inside her blouse sleeve. "Come on. Let's go to the store."

"You know," Georgie said, "we won't have to walk all the way back to my house if we take these little guys with us in the basket."

"To the grocery store?"

"Yeah, why not? They'd be okay. They'd like taking a little trip, instead of being cooped up in that dark old shed."

"But isn't there some kind of law against animals in food stores?" Lynn said uncertainly. "I mean, you never see dogs or cats inside them."

"And nobody will see our mice, either. We'll hide them in the basket. Come on, let's go."

I jumped up. "We're really in business now. Fudge, miracles . . ."

"Wait. We have to end the meeting right." Lynn set down the hoop. We brought it up around us carefully so we didn't smush the little mice crawling around in our blouses.

"We will always be friends, amen, let's *go!*"

Fifteen minutes later we walked into the store. I held the money, Lynn held the list, and Georgie held the basket—with the mice in it again—swinging innocently from her arm.

"I don't know about this," Lynn said in a low voice, for the third time. "I think there's a law . . ."

"The fresh air and exercise will do them good," Georgie said. "Poor little mice, cooped up all day."

"They're not the ones getting the exercise and fresh air," I reminded her. "We are."

"Well, anyway, it'll only take a few minutes to get the sugar and chocolate and stuff. They'll be perfectly safe in the basket. You'll see."

We started hearing *scratch-scratch-scrabble* noises as we passed the dairy aisle. The hinged lid of the wicker basket started bumping up and down as we went by the bread aisle. A little bit of white fur and pink nose poked out about the time we rounded the ice-cream freezer.

"Uh-oh." I stared at the bobbing lid. "They're getting out!"

"Hold it down!" Georgie hissed. We hurried by the freezer section.

Scratch, scratch, scratch. Were the noises as loud as they seemed?

"Somebody's going to notice!" Lynn whispered fiercely. "I told you this was a dumb idea!"

The lid wobbled again. Miracle and Fudge and Saint Francis really wanted out.

"Back here, quick." Georgie pushed us back against the cracker-and-cookie aisle. She reached into the basket and grabbed. "Quick, put 'em in your blouses." She practically threw Miracle at me.

A shopping cart was turning the corner at the far end of the aisle. I pushed Miracle in between the third and fourth buttons of my blouse and quickly shut the opening. He tumbled toward my waist. I checked to make sure my blouse was tucked in all the way around. Georgie dumped Saint Francis down her collar, but there wasn't time for Lynn to get Fudge out before the shopping cart came toward us.

"Chocolate, sugar . . ." I hurried down the aisle, grabbing the ingredients fast and furiously, while little paws scratched and scrabbled around inside my blouse.

"Hey, kids, walk!" yelled a man in a white apron from the meat counter.

"To the checkout. Hurry!" Georgie shoved me from behind.

I tried to stand slouched so that my blouse puffed out to hide the little bump that was moving around and around.

The clerk started ringing up the stuff. There were little scratchy sounds coming from the basket. The lid bumped. Fudge was mad he'd got left inside.

"Hey, isn't it great to be out of school?" I said loudly to Lynn and Georgie.

"Yeah, great!" they yelled back.

Scratch, scratch.

"But you get all next week off," Lynn shouted at me.

"You guys got all *this* week," I yelled back.

The sugar was rung up. And the chocoloate.

Uh-oh. Saint Francis's tail was showing from below Georgie's short-sleeved blouse. I pointed frantically. She reached up and shoved him back, then giggled. He must have crawled someplace ticklish.

The clerk looked at her. Georgie was sort of squirming

around. "Uh, I just got over the measles," she said, twitching a little at the waist. Then, under her breath: "Saint Francis, you get back in there!"

Scratch, scratch. Darn that Fudge.

The clerk was staring at all of us now.

"Here's the money." I shoved the bill at the clerk and poked Georgie. "Go!" I hissed. "Both of you!"

"Bye," said Georgie. "Come on, Lynn." She grabbed Lynn's arm, half walking, half running for the exit.

"Hey—" said the clerk, frowning.

"I need my change, please." My voice sounded desperate. The clerk hadn't bagged anything, so I started throwing things into the bag myself. I tried not to twitch or squirm as little paws worked their way up my back, pit-a-pat, to my collar.

"Hurry, please," I babbled. "I have to get home. My mom's sick. She really needs this chocolate."

Oh, no. The paws were on my braid. Climbing up.

If only I were rich and could say, "Keep the change." It wouldn't even work as a sacrifice, though. You had to give up money to poor people, not grocery clerks.

I reached out and grabbed the money she was still holding in her hand.

"Thanks." My fist closed over it just as the paws reached the top of my braid and started up my scalp.

The clerk's eyes went from my hand to my head.

She yelped.

I bolted for the door. A tail whipped my head with each step.

10

THE NEXT DAY WAS GOOD FRIDAY, THE ONLY
day that I'd be home all day with no parents around. Mom
was taking the week after Easter as vacation, to be home
with me. But not today. Right before Easter was one of the
busiest times at the candy store where she worked.

It was the perfect time to try our fudge making. Georgie
and Lynn came over promptly at one o'clock as we'd
planned.

"Got everything we need right here!" Lynn said excitedly, waving the grocery bag at me. "I hid it under my bed
all night."

I stared at Georgie, who was standing on the porch,
holding a piece of wire screen in one hand and a paper bag
in the other. "What's that for?"

"Penance and sacrifice," Georgie said cheerfully.

"What!"

"Like Saint Francis," she explained, dumping the piece of
screen on the coffee table. "The hair-shirt stuff."

I looked at Lynn. "Do you know what she's talking
about?"

"Would you just listen?" Georgie demanded. "Remember that book about Saint Francis? It said he wore hair shirts and poured ashes over his head."

"But what—"

"*Listen!*" she yelled. "I'm trying to explain! The ashes part was easy. I just dumped my mom and dad's ashtrays into this little bag. But the hair-shirt part was harder." She waved the screen at us. "You *know* there's no way to get real hair shirts. But remember, Robin, you said the idea is to be itchy and scratchy and all. So I figured maybe we could use this screen."

I looked at the bag of ashes and the piece of screen. Sometimes I underestimated old Georgie.

Lynn wasn't impressed. "How do you wear a screen?" she said sarcastically, starting to unpack the grocery bag.

"Well, I thought maybe we could wear strips of screen around our waists, like belts. I'll bet *that* would itch and scratch. And we can dump the ashes on our heads. . . ."

"Stop! You'll get ashes in the fudge stuff!" Lynn yelped, grabbing up the chocolate. "We came over to make fudge, not penance!"

I looked from Lynn, holding her chocolate, to Georgie, waving her screen. They looked as if they were about ready to have a duel. "How about we make the fudge first, in here. And then do the penance and sacrifice out in the club-spot?" I said, trying to make peace.

"Fine. Now we need a big saucepan to cook the fudge in and a baking pan to pour it into." For once Lynn was giving the orders, standing very straight and official at the kitchen counter, reading from her recipe. "It's called 'Heavenly Fudge.' "

"Saint Francis would like that!" Georgie beamed.

"Okay, now we dump all this stuff into the saucepan, then we 'cook it to a soft ball stage.' " She looked up. "Does anybody know what a soft ball stage is? I thought it was supposed to make squares, not balls."

I frowned. "Mom made candy at Christmas, and she dropped little pieces of it on a plate to see if it was ready."

"So you cook it until it looks like a softball?" Georgie sounded amazed.

"I guess so. I'll be in charge of stirring," Lynn said. "Robin, you do the soft-ball dropping . . ."

Lynn sure was being bossy in my kitchen. *My* kitchen. No wonder she wanted to do cooking projects: so she could boss us all around.

"You do the softball!" I glared at her. "I'll do the stirring. It's my spoon."

I stirred. Lynn dropped a spoonful onto a plate, and it splatted all over the counter.

Georgie stirred. Lynn dropped another spoonful, and it splatted again.

Lynn stirred. Georgie dropped a huge spoonful, and it splatted like chocolate rain.

The stuff was bubbling all over the place now.

I stirred. Lynn dropped some more and it sort of stayed together.

"Is that a soft ball?" She squinted at it.

"Looks pretty good to me," Georgie said, licking the spoon.

"Try one more."

Lynn splatted it down.

"That's a better soft ball," I said. "That must be right. Hurry, pour it into the fudge pan. We'll let it set, then—"

"Eat some!" Georgie cut in, grinning.

"No we don't!" I cried. "We have to give it up. This is Good Friday. We should fast."

Georgie opened her mouth. I knew what question was coming.

"Fast means you don't eat. When you *really* fast, you don't eat anything all day. But there's another kind of fast that just means you don't eat desserts or between meals."

"That's the kind we'll do, then."

"And it includes fudge." I looked down at the pan of runny chocolate. "Could be we didn't cook it long enough. . . ."

"It'll harden," Lynn said confidently. "Then we can sell it and make lots of money."

I pulled Georgie away from the pan before she could reach out a finger to lick. "When you're fasting, you can't even lick things. Let's go outside and make our hair shirts."

II

I REALLY HAD UNDERESTIMATED GEORGIE.
She figured out how to make three hair shirts out of that
screen by cutting it into three long belt pieces. And then she
turned the spiky wire ends in, to prickle our waists and
make us itch and scratch even worse. We wrapped them
around us, letting our blouses fall loosely over them to hide
the little bulge. The sharp pieces of metal started jabbing
right away.

"Ooh, ow, this *hurts*!" Lynn adjusted hers gingerly. "I
bet real hair shirts weren't this bad. *Ouch!*"

"Part of the penance is not to complain," I informed her.
"You're supposed to bear your troubles in cheerful silence."

Lynn just sat there, scowling. "We've been doing sacrifices all week! How long is this miracle going to take?"

"Just don't move," Georgie advised. "If you don't move,
it doesn't prickle so bad." She lifted her arm slowly and
picked up the bag. "Now for the ashes. . . . First me, then
Lynn." She poured some over her curly blond hair.

"There better not be any cigarette butts in there," Lynn
muttered. "Why did those saints think it was a good idea
to dump ashes over their heads, anyway?"

"I don't know." I held the bag over my head and shook some out. "Georgie, you've got a big, gray smudge right on your nose."

"Well, your hair's all dirty!" She giggled.

"Come on, let's go see if the fudge is ready."

"Wait, wait!" I reached for the Hula Hoop. "This is our first official cooking day *and* our first fast day, so we should end our meeting right."

It was hard bending over to pull the Hula Hoop around us. The little sharp prickles of screen poked like nails at my skin. Wincing, we pulled the hoop up slowly, carefully.

"We will always be friends, amen." We looked like Halloween hobos with arthritis. I didn't even try to set the hoop down carefully in its usual place behind the garage. Bending over was torture. So I just left it propped in full view against the fence and hurried after Lynn and Georgie, who were moving like stiff robots toward the kitchen.

"Oh, it smells good in here! I'll bet that fudge is hard as—"

"Syrup," Lynn finished in disgust, tipping the pan and watching the whole chocolate mass slide from side to side. "It didn't harden at all!"

"We didn't make a hard-enough softball."

"I know what'll make it hard. The freezer!" I picked up the pan, backing away from the counter as I accidentally bumped my hair shirt and felt the screen jabbing at my skin. "The freezer makes anything hard real quick."

It *didn't* work so quickly. But after an hour or so of waiting, the stuff at least had stopped sliding around when we jiggled the pan. I lifted out a piece that felt more like thick icing than real, chewable fudge. But it *was* chocolaty, creamy, rich-looking. My mouth watered. I'd forgotten to eat lunch. And now I couldn't have anything at all until dinner. Me and my big ideas about fasting.

My hand started moving toward my mouth with the fudge. I shut my eyes, forced my hand back down to the counter.

"I guess . . . this is the piece I sacrifice," I sort of whispered.

Lynn and Georgie did the same with the pieces they'd picked up. After Georgie set hers down, she turned around for a second. I knew she was licking her fingers.

"Hurry, let's sell it before it melts," Lynn said, testing the fudge with her fingers. "It's softer already!"

At first everything went great. "Fudge for sale! Five cents apiece," we announced to whoever answered the door; then we gave it to the person in a little plop on a napkin.

But after two or three houses, the fudge didn't plop anymore, and it was too gooey to pick up, so Georgie ran back to my house to get a spoon.

"Hope they don't mind it by the spoonful," I muttered, when she came back running jerkily.

"This hair shirt is *killing* me," she said, panting.

We tried Mrs. Higgins next. Mrs. Higgins was the perfect grandma-type neighbor. She didn't yell at us if we climbed her fences, and she always had a big, friendly smile for everyone. Once Georgie picked a tomato from Mrs. Higgins's garden, then knocked at her door to ask if she could please have some salt. Mrs. Higgins just smiled and said sure.

"Fudge! My, that does look good," she said, opening her screen door wide. "I'll take two pieces." Then she squinted as we sort of poured some onto a napkin for her. "My . . . my" was all she said, holding the napkin very carefully. And she paid us an extra nickel.

We weren't so lucky at the next house. "You call that fudge?" Eight-year-old Joey Owens laughed.

"It's fudge chocolate sauce," Georgie informed him with great dignity. "They make it this way in Portugal."

"Oh." For a second Joey looked impressed. Then his eyes went from the fudge to the three of us. "You all have dirty faces! I'm not going to eat your fudge. It's probably dirty, too!"

It took a long time to get rid of the whole panful. The grownups didn't want fudge by the spoonful. And most of the little kids playing around the neighborhood didn't have any money.

My hair shirt was digging in worse with each step. My waist felt like it was on fire. I was thirsty and starving. And sick of selling fudge.

"We sure aren't making much money." Lynn shook her coin purse. "We haven't even made enough to pay for the ingredients!"

"This-hair-shirt-is-killing-me." Georgie twisted and squirmed and scowled. "I can't stand it anymore!"

"I'm thirsty."

"Let's go back."

"First we have to get rid of this fudge. Hey!" I waved my hand at nine-year-old Mike Armstrong, playing in the next yard. "You want a real bargain? Go get a nickel, okay?" I scraped up the rest of the fudge and poured it onto a napkin. "There! You can have all our fudge sauce for the price of one little scoop!" I beamed at him, took his nickel, and left him there with chocolate oozing out of the napkin onto his hand and the sidewalk.

The minute we got back to my house I took off my hair shirt. I had to sort of peel it off, slowly, carefully, because the little metal spikes were stuck to my skin in about a hundred different places. My whole waist had a rash.

Georgie and Lynn looked the same.

"Wow," Georgie said. "I bet we could get scabs from these." She touched her rash. "There's *blood* there!"

"Yeah," Lynn said, "and I just thought of something else. If there's rust on these screens, we could get lockjaw and die."

I gulped. I could almost feel my jaw muscles tightening.

It felt so good to get that awful thing off, I just stood there for a minute, not moving, until Lynn's cry made me spin around.

"Our fudge pieces are gone! Someone ate our sacrifices!"

Sure enough the plate was empty, except for some chocolate drips.

Georgie stood there, holding her hair shirt.

"*You* did it, didn't you?" Lynn turned on her. "*You* ate the pieces we sacrificed!"

Georgie opened her mouth and shut it. She looked cornered.

"You did it when you came back for the spoon, I'll bet," Lynn went on angrily. "Didn't you?"

"No!" Georgie yelled back. "I didn't. I don't eat sacrifices!"

"Liar." I knew she'd done it. One look at her face told me.

"Oh yeah?" She turned to me angrily. "Oh yeah? Well, if that's how much you trust me, here's what I think of your stupid sacrifices!" And she threw her hair shirt down on the linoleum. "It'll be *your* fault if I get lockjaw!"

"You brought the screens!"

"Well, this whole stupid sacrifice idea was yours! And I don't want to do it anymore! It's Catholic stuff. And I'm not even Catholic!"

"Oh yeah? You are too! I baptized you!" I glared back.

"It doesn't count, because you used water from the hose and you said you're supposed to use holy water! And I'm not going to do any of your stupid Catholic things anymore. I don't care if the sun dances or not!" And she turned and walked out the door, slamming it hard.

"We don't want you in our club anyway!" I yelled after her. "You . . . you . . . you whited sepulcher!"

Lynn and I looked at each other.

"She ate our fudge all right."

"She's out of our club from now on."

"I'm not even talking to her. Ever again."

Lynn leaned over and picked up the hair shirt and threw

it in the trash. "Come on. We'd better get this mess cleaned up before your mom comes home."

Good Friday was the wrong name. It was bad Friday. Very bad Friday.

It got worse.

12

I WAS STARVING BY SUPPERTIME. NO LUNCH, and then the whole afternoon without snacks. All that tromping up and down the block, all that agony with the hair shirts; then the fight and the clean-up. It took Lynn and me over an hour to make the kitchen look like we hadn't been cooking in it.

Dinner was very late because Mom went shopping after work. Then, just as we were sitting down at the table, there was a knock at the door.

It was Jen. She was wearing a tight, low-cut red dress and high-heeled shoes. Her hair was piled up on her head. She had on loads of makeup. Bright red lipstick. There was a haughty tilt to her head and a cold look in her eyes.

"Jen—" Mom said it almost like a question. "Come in . . ." She turned to Dad, who had sprung out of his chair and was staring at Jen.

A chill ran through me. I took a step back, away from the doorway.

Jen walked in. She sat down in a kitchen chair, crossed her legs, lit a cigarette.

"Why are you staring?" she said to Mom and Dad in a

strange, cold voice. "Sit down." Then, with a little thrust of the chin, "You don't approve of me, do you?" This was aimed at Mom, along with the cigarette smoke. Her eyes narrowed into angry slits.

"Honey," Mom began, "of course I do . . ." Her voice was straining to sound normal; the rest of her was like a high-tension wire pulled taut. She gave Dad an urgent look.

"You don't have to lie," Jen said, snuffing out her cigarette and lighting another one.

The chill inside me was turning to ice. I felt shaky.

It was Jen. And it wasn't Jen. It was Jen's body, and someone else inside. Someone cold and hard. Someone I didn't like.

I didn't want to see this. I took three more steps backward, out of the kitchen, into the hall.

"You never have approved of me. I know that," said the strange Jen in the cold voice from the kitchen.

I ran down the hall and closed my bedroom door, to shut out that strange, awful Jen. I'd stay in here, let Mom and Dad do something with that person out there. They could figure it out and tell me what was going on.

Even with the door shut, though, I could hear the voices. Mom's and Dad's were low, trying to be pleasant, almost as if they were talking to a stranger. But Jen's was getting louder, angrier. I heard swear words, accusations.

Would Mom or Dad try to call Jen's doctor?

I sat on my bed, drew my knees up to my chin, and stared out the window. I'd put my bed against the wall especially because of the window. I liked looking out at the night sky.

It was a clear night. I stared at the stars, at the shadows of the backyard tree.

Jen. What was the matter with her?

The stars blurred. I wiped my eyes.

And then I saw the Hula Hoop. I shouldn't have been able to see it at all in the dark, but the neighbors had left an outside light on and it shone down on the hoop.

The fence was invisible in the dark. The Hula Hoop seemed to hang in midair, a glowing circle of light, like a halo . . .

I squinted. Was it—could it be—really just hanging there? It looked like it. I couldn't see anything behind it. . . .

Was the yellow glow of the Hula Hoop getting brighter? I rubbed my eyes. A different kind of shiver prickled my scalp. I felt dizzy, lightheaded.

A golden circle of light. There in the night sky. For me.

A vision. I knew it. I stared at it, hypnotized. I couldn't keep my eyes off it. The halo light stretched and wavered. I wiped my eyes again.

It *was* a vision! Not even a good-luck Hula Hoop could hang in midair all by itself. Or send out such golden light.

A vision. For me. At last.

"Thank you, God," I whispered. "But God, about that miracle—I've changed my mind. I don't really care if the sun dances. It'd probably mess up the tides, anyway. What I really want is—

"Please—make Jen okay."

13

I KNEW RIGHT AWAY THE NEXT MORNING what needed to be done. I would build a shrine. That's what people always do at places where visions happen. They put statues there, and flowers and even altars, and make them true sacred places. That's what the children of Fatima did.

The house was very quiet. There was a note on the refrigerator:

Dear Robin,

I drove up with Jen to see her doctor. Be back as soon as I can.

Love,
Mom

I felt a little strange going back to the club-spot in cheery broad daylight. It looked very ordinary. Full of weeds, like usual. The Hula Hoop was standing in the weeds at the edge of the club-spot.

Standing in the weeds. There, right there, was my

proof. Proof that a miracle had happened, that the Hula Hoop had appeared to me as a round golden circle in the night. It could not have gotten up from those weeds by itself.

A tingly holy feeling swept over me. I was on holy ground. Should I kneel?

I had to fix this place up, make it look like a real shrine. This couldn't be the club-spot anymore.

I started pulling weeds. I didn't want to clear up the whole place, just a little section at the back where the honeysuckle grew. I'd leave the rest of the place the same, for camouflage. I didn't want anyone else to know about it.

Shrines needed statues. All shrines had them. I ran into the house to get the statue of Our Lady that I'd won last year in school for selling magazine subscriptions. It was white and tall and pretty. And it was made of plastic, so rain wouldn't wreck it.

I set the statue carefully against the honeysuckle. Perfect . . . almost. Most shrines had a sort of altar. . . .

I looked at the Hula Hoop; remembered again how it had looked shining and golden in the night.

A great idea came. I ran to get the shovel and started digging a narrow trench to put the Hula Hoop in, burying the bottom part to keep it standing upright. Then I set the statue inside the hoop.

It looked great! Like a giant halo around the statue. It made the whole place look almost like an altar.

My secret shrine. The Shrine of My Vision. I wouldn't tell Lynn a thing about it. And when Georgie and I were on speaking terms again, I wouldn't tell her, either.

Easter is Miracle Day. Jesus rising from the dead and all. So on Easter morning I made an early visit to my shrine and picked an especially big bouquet from Mrs. Higgins's garden. She had told us we could pick her flowers whenever we wanted. I knelt at my altar. I said a prayer. And when I looked at my Hula Hoop and remembered my vision, that special holy, tingly feeling broke out all over me again.

I knew my prayers were starting to work. Jen had been herself, her usual cheerful, pretty self since she and Mom had gotten back from the doctor. Easter morning she gave me a big chocolate bunny and wore a pretty blue skirt and blouse.

"I like that outfit a lot better than the one you wore Friday," I told her.

She gave me a funny look. "Friday?" she said. "I wasn't here Friday, Robin. You're getting your days mixed up."

I stared at her. "But . . ." I started to argue, then I saw Mom standing behind Jen, shaking her head at me—her "keep quiet" kind of warning look. "Robin, can you help me in the kitchen?" she said.

"Mom," I began, but she put her finger to her lips, hushing me again. Then in the kitchen she said, "Jen really doesn't remember that she came Friday, Robin. She was, uh, sick that day." She turned to the cupboard and started pulling out plates. "So it's best not to mention it again, okay?"

"Sick?" I said, confused. "What do you mean? How come she doesn't remember? I don't get it."

Mom took a deep breath. "It's hard to explain. . . ." The doorbell rang.

"Robin, Lynn's here," Dad yelled.

"Dinner won't be ready for a while. You can go outside." Mom sounded relieved to get rid of me.

I stood there a second longer. "But . . ." I tried again. Then I heard Lynn's voice calling through the screen.

"Robin, come out, quick," she cried. "Georgie's here and she's got bad news!"

"Georgie?" I ran through the door and banged it shut behind me. "Lynn, we're not talking to Georgie, remember?" We'd planned on giving her the silent treatment for a week, at least.

Georgie was standing there on the front lawn, with tears running down her cheeks. "They found our mice," she sobbed. "They made me give back Fudge and Miracle and Saint Francis!" She was gulping and bawling and her face was all red and blotchy. "They made me give them back to Bobby!"

This was not a time for the cold-shoulder silent treatment.

"Who made you give them back!" I cried in horror. "Who found them?"

"Mom and Dad." Georgie gulped out the words.

"But you said your parents never went into the shed," Lynn cried.

"They k-keep the Easter baskets in a b-box in the shed," Georgie bawled. "I t-tried to tell them that m-maybe the Easter Bunny brought us the mice, but they j-just got madder." She wiped her nose on her sleeve. "B-Bobby wouldn't even give me the money back. He said he'd spent it!"

"He did what?"

"The creep!"

"I bet he didn't really spend it! I bet he lied!"

"He gave me these." Georgie dug into her pockets and pulled out some tiny coins. "Bus tokens," she said in disgust. "He probably stole them from his parents."

"Bus tokens?" I stared. "Who needs bus tokens, for Pete's sakes!"

Georgie shrugged, sniffling. "Might as well keep them. We can take a bus trip sometime."

"Well, at least we still have the rest of our money." Lynn plopped down in the grass.

"No we don't," I declared. "We promised to give it up. Remember?"

Georgie opened her mouth, then shut it. I knew what she wanted to say: "Don't give me any more of your Catholic stuff." I could see the words right on her face as she stared at me. I stared right back. I knew I'd win. After all, she'd eaten our fudge. She had to make it up to us to be best friends again. She wasn't in any position to go bossing anyone around right now.

I was right. "Well, not *all* of it, then," she said sullenly, still sniffling. "We have to keep enough for a candy bar or something. We can't just give up *everything*!" She started crying again. "Poor Fudge, poor Miracle, poor Saint Francis. We already had to give *them* up."

Lynn sighed. I could tell she wasn't too crazy about the idea, either. "So how do we give up our money? Who do we give it to?" she asked practically.

"Well . . ." I wasn't sure, exactly. But I didn't want them to know that. I was supposed to be the expert on things like this. "There are lots of places we could take it to. We just have to decide."

"Well, just so long as we save enough for a candy bar," Georgie said. "That's not asking for much—just one little old candy bar."

"Okay." I gave in. She looked so sad, so blotchy and pitiful.

That cheered her up. "Hey, now that we're friends again, let's go to the club-spot and our friendship ring!"

"No," I said quickly. They both looked at me in surprise. "How come?"

"Uh . . ." My mind raced frantically, trying to think of an instant excuse. "Because there's . . . red ants there. They're all over the place, even in the Hula Hoop. There's this tiny crack in it and they crawled in," I babbled. "And, and . . . I have to go back in the house. Jen's here. We're going to have Easter dinner." And I raced toward the porch before

Georgie could say she wanted to see the red ants. "Bye!"

When I walked back in, I heard voices in the kitchen, arguing. I stood, listening. Mom and Dad hadn't talked to me much about Jen. Eavesdropping was about the only way to really find out anything.

"He's going to start me on Sodium Pentothal treatments." Jen's voice came through clearly from the kitchen.

"I don't know about all of this." Mom sounded worried, disapproving.

"It's the only way to find out," Jen said urgently. "I've *got* to. With the Sodium Pentothal, I'll be able to remember back to when I was really young."

"The whole thing's a waste of time and money." Dad's voice was almost a growl. "Jen, these headshrinkers don't know what they're doing half the time. Messing around with all those medicines."

"He's trying to help me! That's what he's doing!"

"Well, it'll take some doing to convince me of that."

"Dad, he said you might not like the idea, might not understand, but that you could meet him, ask him questions, and. . . ."

But Dad wasn't listening anymore. His footsteps came toward the hall. I started trying to look like I was busy instead of eavesdropping.

"Uh, when's dinner?" I asked Dad, instead of the questions I really wanted to ask: "What's Sodium Pentothal? And why does Jen want to remember back to when she was little? What's that got to do with now?"

But Dad hardly even noticed me standing there, he was

so deep in his own thoughts. There was a scowl on his face. Whatever that Sodium Pentothal was, he didn't like it. Mom didn't, either.

Was that doctor good? Was he going to make Jen okay? Or was it going to take something more than that? . . .

I pulled my chocolate bunny out of the box and nibbled off its ear, chewing slowly, letting the smooth chocolate roll around my mouth. Good old Jen, bringing me my favorite kind of solid milk chocolate, even though Mom always got us all chocolate-cream eggs each year.

At least the vision and shrine and sacrifices were doing some good. Jen was better. Anyone could see that. Now I just had to figure out the best way for Lynn and Georgie and me to give up our money.

If we needed a miracle, that would help to bring it.

14

THE IDEA CAME A WEEK LATER, IN RELIGION class. From Sister Agnes Joseph, of all people. She started class that morning by writing the word *pilgrimage* on the board.

"Does anyone know what the word *pilgrimage* means?" Sister asked.

Theresa waved her hand in the air. "It's a trip, isn't it, Sister? A trip to a faraway place or something?"

Sister nodded. "Very good, Theresa. But that's not all there is to a pilgrimage. A pilgrimage, boys and girls, is a *holy* trip, to a sacred place. The people who make these holy trips are called *pilgrims.*" She waved her pointer with each word. "Long ago, pilgrims would fast during the whole trip, or crawl partway on their hands and knees as a penance, or go barefoot over rocks. Sick people came, hoping to be cured; or others made the journey to pray for them. They brought gifts to the shrines: money, valuables. And, boys and girls, such pilgrimages were not made only by *Catholics.* People of all religions make pilgrimages to sacred places: Jews, Hindus, Muslims . . ."

I sat up straight in my seat, listening hard, staring at the word on the blackboard. *Pilgrimage.* A trip . . . to ask for someone to get well . . . bringing money . . .

Perfect.

I could hardly wait to tell Lynn and Georgie. The three of us would go on a pilgrimage.

"No more Catholic stuff," Georgie said stubbornly. She folded her arms and glared at me. "I *told* you."

"But it's not just Catholic," I broke in eagerly. "Sister says everyone goes on pilgrimages: Protestants, Jews, even Hindus! It's a very popular thing to do!"

Lynn leaned back against the tree, chewing on a piece of grass. "But you said those pilgrims went hundreds of miles, up mountains and stuff. We can't do that! I don't want to do that."

"And, anyway," Georgie added, "there aren't any holy places around here."

"Sure there are. Churches," I said. "We don't have to go hundreds of miles. We could pick a church that's a couple of miles away. Saint Ignatius is too close and too ordinary. That wouldn't count as a real pilgrimage. But if we picked a church that's farther away, we could walk there and leave our money. . . ."

"And go buy our candy bar," Georgie said. "Pick a church that's near a store."

"Well, as long as we buy it *after* we go to church," I said. "Pilgrims are supposed to fast."

Lynn and Georgie both groaned. "Not that penance and

sacrifice stuff again," Georgie declared. "I am *not* going to wear any hair shirt! I threw mine away."

"Me, too," Lynn said, siding with Georgie. "I'm not wearing one, either."

"Look," I said in my most agreeable, persuasive voice. "You've got the wrong idea about this. It's an adventure, an exciting trip. We can even go barefoot. Pilgrims are supposed to."

"Yeah?" Georgie looked more interested.

"We can't just walk there the easy way, though," I went on. "Pilgrimages are supposed to be hard trips. So we shouldn't use the sidewalk."

"Oh, I get it!" Georgie cried. "Like a safari!" She jumped up. "I'll plan our pilgrimage! I could plan a good trip without using the sidewalk even *once.*"

"I don't know . . ." I said. Georgie didn't really know much about things like this. She didn't have any religious education, after all.

Her chin lifted stubbornly. "I plan it, or I don't go!"

"Okay! But remember, we're supposed to end up at a church."

"Right," she nodded cheerfully. "I'll even make a map."

"We can go Saturday!"

"I'll bring our money."

"No shoes."

"We should get the Hula Hoop," Lynn said excitedly. "This is like a regular club meeting."

"It's still full of red ants," I said, not looking at her. "I guess we'd better forget about it and use something else. The whole club-spot is just crawling with ants."

"Too bad." Lynn sighed. "Well, we could hold hands and make a ring."

We joined hands solemnly.

"We will always be friends. Saturday's our pilgrimage. Amen."

15

"HERE IT IS!" GEORGIE WAVED A PIECE OF crumpled paper in front of me. "It'll be the greatest pilgrimage that ever was! We'll fence-walk the neighborhood, starting at Lynn's back wall, then climb onto the Duncans' flat garage roof, then back down to the Perkinses' fence, through the Warners' backyard, and out through their back gate to the street! And that's just the first part!" She beamed at Lynn and me.

"Hey, that sounds great!" I looked from the paper, full of lines and squiggles, to Georgie's eager face. "But we *are* going to end up at a church, right?"

"Have you no faith?" Georgie grinned. "Of course we're going to end up at a church! Just leave it to me."

Lynn peered at the map over my shoulder. "How are we going to walk those fences and things barefoot?" she protested. Lynn didn't like fence walking and tree climbing much, even with shoes on. "We'll kill our feet!"

Georgie shrugged. "Pilgrims suffer," she said. "Right, Robin?"

"Yeah, right. Pilgrims bring money, too." I pulled the money out of my pocket. It was tied up in a handkerchief.

It seemed more pilgrimlike that way. "We're all set. Let's get going. I have to be home by lunchtime." Mom had been busy sorting laundry when I told her I was going for a walk with Lynn and Georgie. She hadn't asked questions, thank goodness.

"Onward, pilgrims!"

Lynn's place wasn't too bad barefoot. It was cement block, with nice wide places to walk on. The gritty roughness wasn't bad enough to really hurt. It was too bad we weren't making this pilgrimage in summer, after our feet were already toughened up; then there'd be no problem at all.

"It's a good thing our television's in the front room," Lynn whispered as we edged along the wall, trying to keep low. "Everyone in my family's watching Saturday-morning cartoons. Otherwise, they'd be sure to see us up here."

Georgie was already at the end of Lynn's wall, pulling herself onto the Duncans' garage roof.

"Oof," she gasped, wriggling up on her belly. She reached out a hand to help pull me up.

"Wait for *me*!" Lynn called in a loud whisper. "Don't go so darn fast!" Poor Lynn. She wasn't so good at this sort of thing. Too afraid of cutting her hands or tearing her clothes, even if she was wearing jeans.

I'd had a hard time deciding if it would be okay to wear jeans. Usually, to be dressed properly for church, you needed to wear a dress and, of course, shoes. But I figured there were different rules for pilgrims. You just couldn't climb all those hard places in a dress. Those long-ago pilgrims probably wore old clothes when they crawled up mountains and stuff, too.

"Wait!" Lynn called again.

"Shhh!" Georgie hissed. "Do you want the whole neighborhood to know we're here?"

It took both of us to get Lynn up onto the garage roof. She lay there, panting, brushing dirt from her feet.

"So what's next on your dumb map?" She scowled.

Georgie consulted her paper. "Across this roof, *quietly.* Because if anyone's home, he could hear us walking."

We tiptoed carefully across the black, pebbly surface. A dog started barking in the other yard.

"Rats," Lynn hissed. "Now someone will come out for sure. *Hurry!*"

"Just one last fence and we can jump down," Georgie said, lowering herself off the roof, feeling with her feet for the fence below. The hard kind—chain link. I could see her toes curling into the holes in the fence, grabbing for a hold.

"Great," Lynn muttered behind me. "Chain link fence. Just great."

You can't just walk across a chain link fence. You have to cling to it like a monkey in a cage, moving across toehold by toehold, fingerhold by fingerhold.

"No jumping down," Georgie hissed, as if she could read my mind. "Pilgrims can't cheat. We have to cross the whole way without touching the ground, or it doesn't count."

I tried to make my fingers and toes move faster along the

chain link. Each link seemed to dig deeper into my skin.

"This fence is killing my feet." Lynn looked like she'd had it. "I'm going to fall any second!"

"You're almost there," Georgie called encouragingly. "And if you had shoes on, you'd never be able to get your toes into the fence to hold on. . . ." Her last words sort of disappeared into thin air as she hauled herself onto the next wall—another cement block one—and then jumped down into the adjoining yard. "Hurry, the coast is clear," she whispered up to us.

I breathed a long, grateful sigh of relief, as my fingers grabbed the last edge-pole of the chain link fence. Made it.

"Come on, Lynn. You can do it," I called back, hoisting myself onto the next wall. Ah, wonderful cement block. I lay there a second, relaxing my fingers and toes, then reached down to help Lynn.

"Hurry, *hurry*!" Georgie sounded panicky down in the yard. "Someone's coming!"

I jumped down, practically pulling Lynn with me.

"Hey, you kids! Get out of my yard!" It was Mrs. Warner, standing by the back door, with a rug in her hand. "Get out of here right now, you hear?" She shook the rug at us. "Or I'll call your parents!"

We raced across her yard, plunging through the back gate to the traffic of Sycamore Avenue.

"M-Made it," Georgie gasped. "Oh boy, that was a close one."

Lynn plopped down right on the edge of the curb. Her

face was red, her eyes were smoldering mad, even her shoulders looked angry.

"I scratched my arm. I ripped my blouse. I've got a million pieces of rock in the bottom of my foot." Her voice was slow, quiet, furious. She glared up at Georgie. "So what other tortures have you planned for this lovely pilgrimage?"

"A surprise!" Georgie winked, then dug into her pocket and pulled out three tiny coins. Bus tokens. "The rest of our pilgrimage is by bus!"

"What!" I forgot my aching feet and scrambled back up. "Bus! Pilgrims don't go by bus!"

"Yes they do," Georgie said. "And what do you know—here comes one right now!" She leaned into the street, shading her eyes with her hand. "Wow, I can't believe this timing. It's terrific!"

"But . . . but . . ." Somehow I'd lost control of this pilgrimage. It was rushing along at its own speed, with Georgie at the wheel.

Did she know her way around town? Did she know where the churches were? And did she have enough tokens for the trip home, too?

Georgie stood in the street, waving her arms to flag down the big bus as it rumbled closer. It screeched to a stop by the curb.

"Come on, let's get on." She reached down an arm to yank Lynn up.

The driver stared at us as we climbed on.

"No shoes . . ." he began.

"We're on a pilgrimage," Georgie interrupted him, speaking with great dignity. "Pilgrims do not wear shoes." And before he could say anything else, she dropped our tokens in.

"Sure, sure." He scowled. "And I'm Joan of Arc." But he didn't order us off, just scowled again and pulled away from the curb.

"Whew, another close one," Georgie whispered, plopping into a seat.

I wasn't listening. I was watching our familiar neighborhood whiz by, disappearing into the distance as the bus took us farther and farther down Sycamore Avenue.

"Georgie, do you know where we're going?" I shook her arm. "Do you know where the church is?"

"It's right here." She pulled out her map and jabbed her finger on an X marked at the end of a long red pencil line. There were no street names on the map. Just that pencil line.

"But, where *is* it?"

She wiggled her nose a little and stared out the window. "I'm not sure, exactly. But it's a really old church. I saw it from the car two days ago, when Mom drove me back from the dentist. It's on this street somewhere. . . ."

Lynn moaned and flopped back in the seat. "Great. Just great. We're on our way to some church and we don't even know where it is!" Then suddenly she sat straight up and grabbed Georgie's other arm. "Hey, you *do* have tokens for the trip back, don't you?"

"Well . . . no," Georgie said. "Bobby only gave me three, remember?"

"Great," Lynn said in exactly the same voice, flopping back again. "Just great."

We were still on Sycamore Avenue, but now nothing looked familiar. Out the window I saw some office buildings and apartment houses. Then all of a sudden Georgie jumped up and started yanking madly on the overhead pull cord. "Stop, stop," she cried. "There it is! The big old church! I knew it was on this street!"

"All right!" the driver called back. "Let go of the pull cord, kid!" He swung the bus to the curb. "Good thing you're getting off," he muttered as we climbed down, "or I'd throw you off."

The bus pulled away and we stood in our bare feet at the busy intersection, with cars rushing by on all sides.

"There," Georgie said dramatically, pointing at a big stone church across the intersection. "That's the church I marked on my map. We've reached the end of our pilgrimage!"

16

THE CHURCH WAS VERY OLD. A SPANISH-TYPE building with stucco walls and a red tile roof. A big statue outside. The sign out front said OUR LADY OF MERCY.

We walked slowly toward the huge front door. Suddenly I felt scared, worried, nervous, unsure. The idea had sounded fine when I was sitting on the front lawn, planning this with Lynn and Georgie. But now, standing in front of this holy church in my jeans and dirty blouse and bare feet . . .

Could I really get up the nerve to go in?

"Let's try a side door," I whispered. We could open it just a crack, and if there were other people inside, we could stay outside. I shut my eyes in a silent prayer: Please God, don't let there be any priests or nuns around.

Slowly, cautiously, heart thumping, I pulled at the heavy side door and peered in through the tiny crack.

"What's in there?" Georgie tried to see over my shoulder. "Is it safe? Anyone inside?"

"I don't know. Too dark to see." I pulled the door open a tiny bit more and gazed into the silent, heavy darkness.

No noise at all. So maybe it was empty. Maybe it was safe for us to make a real quick visit. Maybe . . .

I put my finger to my lips. "Shhh," I cautioned. "Be real quiet. Follow me."

We slipped inside, hardly daring to breathe, then stood by the wall a second, waiting for our eyes to adjust.

Heavy, dark pews, big statues on all the walls, a huge altar, a great, high vaulted ceiling—this was much older and more holy and dignified than St. Ignatius Church. This place felt like saints lived here.

A good place to make a pilgrimage to—and to ask for a miracle.

And a terrible place to be found barefoot.

I scuffed my toes on the carpet and gulped. "Well, here we are," I whispered.

"Wow," Georgie breathed, staring at the statues, the altar. "It sure feels holy in here."

"Where do we put the money?" Lynn's voice was a tiny squeak.

"I, I . . ." and then I pulled back quickly against the wall, grabbing Lynn and Georgie with me. There was someone on the far side of the church—an old woman, kneeling by the rows of little votive candles. I shrank closer against the wall, watching as she stood up and lit one of the candles, then dropped a coin into the bowl and left the church by the front entrance, moving slowly.

The candles! We could light a candle and leave our money there in the donation bowl!

"Come on. Follow me," I said in my most reverent hushed voice. "We can light a candle."

I tiptoed across the width of the church, with Georgie and Lynn like silent shadows behind me. It's easy to move quietly in bare feet.

"There're matches here, and lots of candles," I said in a low voice. "You can pick which candle you want to light and then put the money in the bowl."

"That one," Georgie whispered, pointing to the only one not lit in the top row. "I'll do it."

"No. I'll light it." I picked up the match quickly, before she could beat me to it. I used one of the already lit candles to light my match, then I touched it to the top candle and watched it flare into a single bright yellow dancing flame.

"There," I whispered proudly. "Now we leave the money and beat it out of here."

We dumped out the handkerchief into the donation bowl. The coins clinked alarmingly against each other.

"Don't forget to save some for candy bars," Georgie hissed loudly in my ear.

"And what about bus fare?" Lynn added.

I looked at them. "If we take bus money *and* candy-bar money, there won't be anything left. Which should it be?"

"Candy," said Georgie.

"Bus," said Lynn, putting her hands on her hips.

"Candy!" Georgie said, louder. "Look, we can walk home. It's not that far."

"In bare feet?" Lynn hissed.

I looked at our money, all mixed up with everyone else's

in the bowl. I wasn't even sure how much we'd dumped in. And if anyone walked into the church right now and saw us standing there barefoot, in jeans, and taking money *out* of the bowl . . . I started sweating.

There was a tiny sound at the back of the church.

"Oh no—someone's coming!" I grabbed a few dimes and pulled Georgie's arm. "Let's get out of here! Fast!" And I raced back across the church, feeling more like a criminal than a pilgrim, pulling Georgie and Lynn with me, back out through the heavy side door, letting it slam behind us. Then I leaned against the church wall, breathing hard, clutching my dimes and blinking in the sunlight.

"Three thousand four hundred and two steps left to go." Lynn moaned the words. "Three thousand four hundred and one, three thousand four hundred—"

"Shut up," Georgie said. "You're making up those stupid numbers. It's not even that far."

"I'm going to need two new feet by the time we get home." I winced each time the raw, tender underside of my foot hit the sidewalk. "I don't think my feet are going to make it."

"And not even a candy bar," Georgie muttered. "Not even a lousy *store*!"

"That's your fault," I reminded her. "You made up our pilgrimage plan. You had the bright idea of taking the bus."

"Forget candy bars," Lynn moaned. "What I need is a nice cold, tall glass of Coke. Or root beer. Or lemonade." She shaded her eyes with her hand, staring down the boulevard. "At least I'm starting to recognize things. That's Elm Street ahead. Must still be about three thou—"

"*Shut up!*" Georgie shouted.

Never in my entire life had my feet hurt like this. I didn't know it was possible for feet to hurt so much. They'd been through everything—hot pavement, pebbly blacktop, rough weedy lots, chain link fences. Each step felt like stepping into a frying pan, even though the sidewalk here wasn't hot. My feet were just permanently on fire.

We didn't even talk for the next ten blocks. Lynn stopped counting steps. We didn't take the extra steps needed to walk by the drugstore and get candy or pop with our thirty cents. We just kept plodding along, one sore foot ahead of the next.

We got to Lynn's house first.

Lynn turned to me before she started up her driveway. She spoke in a very slow, calm voice. "Robin McCord, if you *ever* say *one word* to me again about anything religious, about sacrifice or penance or pilgrimages or *anything* like that ever again, I'm going to . . . spit in your face!"

Wow. She must have been really fed up. Usually Lynn was more ladylike than that.

Well, she wasn't the only one who was tired and sore and grouchy. And this whole trip was Georgie's planning, not mine. If I'd had the energy, I would have said so. But I didn't. So I just glared at her indignantly.

"Oh, go soak your head," I said.

"Your feet, too," Georgie said with a giggle. "Soak both together, Lynn. You'll need two pails."

The corners of Lynn's mouth turned up the tiniest bit. I felt a giggle coming, too. I turned away so Lynn wouldn't see.

"Bye," I said huffily. She could spit in her own face. That thought made me want to giggle even more. I stomped away toward my own house, leaving Georgie to head toward her end of the block.

Nothing had ever looked so comforting and wonderful as the sight of my house, with its soft green lawn, with that lovely bathtub inside where I could lie down and go to sleep in warm, soft, soothing water. . . .

I hoped God appreciated all this effort.

Of course, you couldn't exactly tell Almighty God that He *owed* you something—but after today, after this long, hard pilgrimage, the sacrifices, the money, the candle, my *feet* . . . Well, it sure seemed like He owed me at least a *little* miracle.

In the Park

I was really a little kid back then. All that sacrifice game stuff with Lynn and Georgie. Making a pilgrimage into an obstacle course.

I feel a whole lot older now today, rolling this Hula Hoop along in the park. It's getting sort of foggy. I've been going very slowly, and I'm only about halfway through the park. I'm still hanging on to the Hula Hoop.

Thinking back to *then* is so much easier than thinking of *now:* The gun. Jen. The hospital. Whenever I think of *now,* I get this quick, sharp pain right through my middle. So I'll keep walking and thinking back . . . That next year, in seventh grade, I wasn't so sure about miracles.

Part 3

Seventh Grade

17

"YOU KNOW," I SAID TO JEN, "IF YOU SPRAY-paint macaroni gold and stick it on cardboard, it makes a real nice, shiny decoration."

"Oh?" said Jen with a little smile, as if she thought it was a funny idea. "I guess that would be . . . shiny." She kept on winding pine branches around the wreath frame on the table. "Me, I like natural things, like this wreath. Doesn't it just *smell* like Christmas?"

She had so many pine branches lying around, ready to be made into decorations, that the whole place did smell like Christmas.

"Isn't macaroni natural?" I asked. I liked gold macaroni. I thought it looked elegant.

This time she laughed out loud. "Not really." She twisted a red ribbon around and around, making a professional-looking bow. "There." She held it up proudly. "If Mom and Dad insist on having a fake tree, at least there'll be some real evergreens in the house, Robin." She grinned at Mom, who was sitting at her desk in the corner of the living room writing Christmas cards.

"Would you quit picking on our poor tree," Mom said

good-naturedly. "It's a nice tree. It doesn't drop needles, and we don't have to shop all over town for it."

"It's okay, if you like plastic."

They were both grinning. They had this fight every year. It was a Christmas tradition, like eggnog. It had to be kept up, even though Jen didn't live here anymore.

"It's in the same category as gold macaroni," Jen said, winking at me.

I kept sticking my macaroni to my cardboard stubbornly.

"You see, Robin"—Jen plopped down in the chair and tucked her feet under her—"things like wreaths mean something. They have for hundreds of years. I've been learning about all these traditions at college. A lot of the things we do at Christmas we got from the pagans."

"We got Christmas from the pagans?" I put my hands on my hips. "You'd better not let Sister Agnes Joseph hear you say that. She'll excommunicate you from the church!"

Sister Agnes Joseph had been teaching for so long, even Jen had had her, way back in grade school.

"Well, it's true." Jen grabbed a handful of Chex Mix and started munching. "Like the wreath. See, the whole idea of having Christmas in December is because it's midwinter, when the days are the shortest and the sun is lowest in the sky. In the old, pagan days, people brought evergreens inside because they were always green. They stood for life. People thought that would help the sun to get higher in the sky again and help spring come." She turned to Mom. "Hey, wouldn't that make a nice Christmas card? A bright green wreath on the front, and instead of those sappy verses, it could say"—she tapped her chin thoughtfully with a pine branch—" 'Evergreen! New life. New hope.' How about that?"

"I thought we used evergreens because there were Christmas trees growing outside the stable where Jesus was born." I had this nice cozy picture in my mind: the stable surrounded by softly falling snow, wise men tiptoeing up and trimming the tree as they went by with their camels, a few reindeer in the distance . . .

"Those kinds of trees don't even grow in Bethlehem," Jen said scornfully.

"Well, I guess Sister Agnes Joseph never went to your college," I said. "She didn't tell us about any of that."

I held up my macaroni piece. "You see this macaroni?" I said with what I thought was great dignity. "It's been around for thousands of years. The Egyptians used it in their squiggly writing. Hiero—hiero—"

"Hieroglyphics, you idiot." Jen threw a couch pillow at me. "And the Egyptians never heard of macaroni, believe me."

I giggled.

It was a great day. Our living room looked like a Christmas card, with Jen sitting there in her red ski sweater, and the fireplace going, the tree lights twinkling, Mom at the desk writing cards. Things were great. Jen was great. She'd come home early for the Christmas holidays. She was helping us get the house all fixed up.

"I just got the greatest idea!" Jen bounced on the couch. "I could have a Christmas party and call it 'Midwinter

Festival.' Like in the pagan days: We could . . . let's see, what would you do at a midwinter festival . . ." She stared thoughtfully at her pine branches. "We could have a 'hanging of the greens' and sing old English carols and have ale or something—" She laughed. "Wouldn't that be an original party?"

"Yoo-hoo! Anybody home?" Georgie's voice called in from the front door. "Wow!" She stepped over the branches, ribbons, scissors, and wire. "Are you guys going into business selling wreaths or something?"

"Jen's making our Christmas nice and pagan," Mom said very matter-of-factly from her desk.

"Oh," Georgie said with a nod. "That's nice."

Jen and I both laughed. Georgie didn't even know what pagan meant. I could tell.

"Georgie, your hair looks cute," Jen said approvingly.

"Thanks." Georgie was a little shy around Jen. She thought Jen was the prettiest person in California.

I stared at Georgie's hair, too. I hadn't really seen her much after school lately. She'd been helping out at her parents' restaurant.

When had her frizzy blond mass turned into a bouncy, cute flip? Jen was right. It did look good.

Jen was staring at me now. A thoughtful, scheming look. "Robin," she said slowly, "why don't we do something different with *your* hair?"

"Huh?" I looked up suspiciously. "Like what?"

"Well . . ." She got up and walked around me, fingering my ponytail. "Cut it, like say shoulder length . . ."

"What! Chop off my ponytail!"

"Great idea!" Georgie was grabbing at my poor ponytail now, too. "Oh, Robin, you'd look so cute!"

"It might be fun to try something new, Robin." Even Mom was joining in.

I looked at Georgie's nice bouncy flip. I looked at Jen's fluffy, shoulder-length hair. I felt my own long, straight ponytail.

"Well . . ." I said, and gulped. "Just don't cut it *too* short. . . ."

The next thing I knew I was in a chair in the bathroom, with a towel around my shoulders and my hair clipped into sections. Jen was standing over me with the scissors, while Georgie perched on the edge of the tub, cheering us on.

Jen held up the scissors.

"Ow!" I jumped. Georgie shrieked.

"Robin!" Jen said sternly. "Georgie. Control yourselves. It does not hurt to cut hair."

"Yes it does." I gulped. It even hurt to hear the scissors come toward me like long crocodile teeth—*snip, snap*—toward my hair that had taken years to grow.

"Jen . . . I changed my mind."

"It'll look *good*, Robin. Now don't chicken out, you hear?" she said in her bossy, big-sister voice. "Where's that old spirit of adventure?"

"It's in my ponytail."

She held up the scissors again.

"Oh, Robin, you're so brave," Georgie whispered, watching wide eyed. "Oh, I can't bear to look!" She covered her eyes as the crocodile teeth made their attack. *Snip, swish.* Hair sailed down all over me. I swallowed once. I swallowed twice. Something was stuck in my throat. My stomach.

"Oh, Robin, there goes the back!" Georgie peeked out through the fingers covering her eyes.

"Shut up," I said. More long hair floated down.

"Georgie," Jen said sweetly, "why don't you tell Robin how nice it's going to look?"

Georgie uncovered her eyes and put her hand on my arm. "It's going to look great, Robin," she said obediently.

"Thanks," I said.

Jen kept cutting with quick, confident snips. It was hard to see the linoleum anymore; the bathroom floor was wall-to-wall hair. My stomach hurt.

"There!" Jen set down the scissors with a nod. "Finished." She handed me the mirror.

I saw a face with short, unfluffy hair. Ugly, straight, short hair. The face looked pale, in shock.

"Uh . . ." I couldn't quite get words out. I opened my eyes wide, to make room for the water that was filling them. I couldn't let it spill out. I couldn't let Jen see.

But she was busy getting out curlers. "Now we have to set it." She stuck some bobby pins in her mouth and sectioned off more hair.

"Oh, Robin, you're so brave," Georgie said again, in a breathless voice. As if I'd just climbed the Alps or something. Well, that's how I felt: like I'd just climbed the Alps—and fallen all the way back down.

Jen rolled my hair in a million curlers and set the hood of her hair dryer over the whole bristly mess.

Forty-five minutes later, a face surrounded by soft, fluffy hair stared back at me from the mirror. When I shook my head, it all sort of bounced on my scalp. Even my head felt light and fluffy. I'd never realized my ponytail was so heavy.

"Oh, Robin!" Georgie shrieked, dancing around me. "It's so cute! Oh, Robin, it's so *cute!*"

"Yep," Jen agreed proudly. "You're a new woman, Robin." She gave me a pleased, big-sister smile.

"Oh, Robin, it's *so cute!*"

I felt like a new person; like the old Robin had fallen to the floor with the old hair. I stood up carefully, hardly daring to move my head, to make any movement that would wreck my great new fluffy hair.

"Now what you need is a cute new outfit," Jen declared. She looked from me to Georgie, then back again.

"Tell you what," she said slowly. "How about you two coming to visit me? Easter vacation, maybe. When spring break starts. We could go shopping and I'll take you out to lunch. Then I could drive us all home. Would you like to do that?"

"Really?" we both cried.

"That'd be great!"

"Can Lynn come, too?"

"You are *so* lucky to have a sister like Jen," Georgie said to me as she got ready to leave. "She's the neatest sister there ever was. When I grow up, I'm going to look just like her."

"No you aren't. I am," I told her smugly.

I was, too. I checked the mirror about twenty-five times that night, and it seemed to me that the last five or six times, when I had lipstick on, there was a definite resemblance.

Before I climbed into bed I looked out my window toward the place behind the garage, where my shrine was hidden. I didn't go there very much anymore. Only once in a while, when I saw an especially nice winter flower somewhere. I'd pick it and set it by the statue of Our Lady.

Funny thing about statues; they really can make a place look holy and sacred. Even a weedy, ugly place like the club-spot. I still felt holy when I went there, even if I couldn't remember anymore how my vision had looked; couldn't really *see* the glowing hoop in my mind.

But Sister was always saying that people should pray to God when things are going well, not just when things are awful. Otherwise, it's selfish, Sister said.

So I sat there on my bed, elbows on the sill, my head full of the good feeling of today and my new hair and Christmas.

Things were going *great*. They really were. Did that mean a miracle had happened?

"Thanks," I whispered to the darkness, just in case.

18

EASTER VACATION. *FINALLY.* AND THE DAY OF
the promised shopping trip with Jen.

"I almost didn't get to come," Lynn said for the third
time. "I thought I was going to *die* when Mom said she
needed me to babysit the bratlets." That's what she always
calls her twin sisters, Connie and Carrie. She pushed Georgie's doorbell. "I had to pull a crying scene and everything."
She pushed the doorbell again. "She *finally* said yes. My eyes
aren't still red, are they?"

"Nope." My mom had almost backed down, too. But I
didn't want to talk to Lynn about that.

"I'm not sure this bus trip to Jen's is such a good idea
right now," Mom had said, just a week ago. "Jen's had a
little setback. Lent," she'd murmured, half to herself.
"Seems like Lent's hooked up to her problem somehow. She
gets worse during the Lent season . . ."

"But you said her doctor's been helping her," I'd argued.
"And that Georgie and Lynn and I would cheer her up. You
know Jen loves shopping, Mom. We'll have a great time.
She'll feel worse if we don't come. Please?" I couldn't stand

to have to tell Georgie and Lynn that our big trip was off. *"Please?"*

So Mom had finally agreed. It was the idea of cheering Jen up that did it. That and the fact that there'd be three of us together.

But I couldn't tell Lynn any of that. Never ever.

"Where *is* Georgie?" Lynn held her thumb over the buzzer. "Georgie," she called through the screen. "We'll miss the bus!"

"Here I come!" We heard a clomping sound across the floor.

Georgie opened the door and stepped down on the porch, wobbling.

She was wearing high heels. She had on lipstick and mascara and face makeup. Her hair was done up on her head. She looked practically ready for high school.

Lynn and I stared at her.

"Like my new heels?" She stuck her foot out proudly. "I just got them to match this skirt. Good thing Mom's gone. She'd never have let me get so dressed up." She started walking across the porch with great grown-up dignity, except for her ankles, which were wobbling all over the place.

"Are you *sure* you want to walk to the bus station in those?" She didn't look like she could walk to the edge of the porch without her ankles caving in.

"Oh sure. No problem."

Lynn and I set the pace, walking as fast as we could with Georgie teetering along beside us.

"There's the bus!" Georgie yelped. Then she reached up to smooth her hair. "Now remember, you guys, act *mature*. We don't want the driver to think we're just little kids."

"Right," we agreed, standing very straight, trying to look dignified and grown-up, as though we caught buses to big cities every day.

We climbed up the steps with great dignity, except for Georgie's heels getting stuck in the groove of the step, making her almost topple back into the street. She caught herself by grabbing Lynn's blouse.

We nodded graciously to the driver as we handed him our tickets and found seats.

Georgie poked me.

"That boy up there. In the blue jacket," she whispered with a little giggle. "Isn't he cute?"

Oh, brother. I rolled my eyes at Lynn. Boy-crazy Georgie. It had started happening a few months ago and it got worse all the time.

"I bet he's even in the high school." There was awe in her voice.

I sighed.

Georgie squirmed a little. "It's kind of crowded here," she said. "I think I'll move up a few seats." She got up and teetered her way along the bus aisle, to the seat opposite the boy.

"Traitor," I muttered after her.

"Deserter," Lynn hissed.

Georgie ignored us the whole rest of the trip. Before three blocks had gone by, she was talking and giggling with the blue-jacket boy. By the time we got on the main highway, she was sitting next to him. Good thing this wasn't a cross-country trip.

"Serve her right if we don't even tell her where to get off," I said to Lynn.

"Yeah."

This bus trip sure was a lot different from our pilgrimage bus ride. Then we'd all three been a team, together, on a big adventure. Barefoot.

And now . . . here was Georgie in her high heels, giggling with that boy.

She finally came back to us just before we got to the bus station where we were meeting Jen.

"His name's Mike," she whispered, grinning like an imbecile. "He's in seventh grade, like us."

We just glared at her.

"Traitor," I said again.

Georgie sighed. "I don't know what it is about boys," she said apologetically. She leaned back in the seat with her eyes half-closed and sighed again. "It's like they're magnets, see, and I'm . . . I'm just a little old piece of iron."

Lynn and I rolled our eyes.

But I forgot about Georgie's treason when I saw Jen standing by the bus station, waiting for us. Smiling, waving.

I hadn't even realized till then that I'd been just a tiny bit worried. But seeing Jen, something inside me breathed a big sigh of relief. It was okay. Mom had been worried for nothing. Jen looked fine. We'd all have a great day on the town!

19

WE BUZZED ALL OVER DOWNTOWN LONG
Beach in Jen's little red VW. We hit the best clothing stores,
took tons of clothes into the fancy dressing rooms, tried
them all on, preened in front of the big mirrors, and let Jen
tell us what looked good.

"I *love* this blouse!" Georgie stared at herself in a soft
chiffon blouse. "I want it!"

"Oh yeah?" Lynn held up the price ticket attached to the
sleeve and waved it in Georgie's face. "Are you sure about
that, Georgie?"

"Yikes!" Georgie sucked in her breath. Her eyes got
huge. "Forty-nine ninety-five for one measly blouse?" she
whispered in awe. She started undoing the buttons, fast.

"This isn't so expensive." Lynn studied herself in the
mirror, turning this way, then that way in a gingham dress.
"Only I can't afford it," she ended sadly. "If they paid me
what they should for baby-sitting the bratlets, then I could
afford the whole store."

"Good clothes cost more," Jen said, zipping up a pair of
yellow slacks. "But they look better and they last longer.
It's worth the money."

"Not if you don't have it to start with," I said, taking one last look at myself in a beautiful pink skirt.

"But *they* don't know we're poor," Georgie aimed her thumb toward the dressing room door. "So why not have fun? I'm going to get ten more things to try on!"

"Me, too!" Lynn started after her. "Hey, let's try on some of those fancy prom dresses!"

The salesladies never would have let us get away with it by ourselves. But Jen wowed them all. The way she thanked them so courteously when she handed back the clothes we'd finished trying on; the way she looked so important in her skirt and jacket; the way she walked, talked—they knew she had class. They would never have suspected in a million years that Jen was as poor as the rest of us. They said, "Shall we show the young ladies this line of dresses?" They didn't even glare at us when we walked out with just one new blouse after we'd tried on half the store. They just smiled and wrapped the blouse and said, "Come again."

"You bet!" Georgie called back, waving and wobbling.

"This is fun!" Jen exclaimed as we headed down Pine Avenue. "I've really been looking forward to you kids coming. Are you ready to eat yet?"

"*Yes!*"

"There's a nice place about three blocks up. We should walk, though. It's impossible to find parking."

"Three blocks," Georgie groaned. She was teetering worse and worse on her heels. "Ugh. I don't think I can make it. My poor blisters . . ."

"You know, this is really fun!" Jen said again. "I've really been looking forward to this."

I looked at her quickly. A little buzz of warning went off. Maybe because she'd said the same thing in the exact same tone, like a recording, with that same bright smile on her face, or maybe because she acted like she hadn't even heard Georgie. Or maybe because in that one quick, hard glance, it looked to me like her smile was stretched over something else not so cheery.

We kept on walking, with Georgie hanging on to both of us for support.

"Ow, ooh, ouch," she moaned. "On the way home I'm going barefoot. Why didn't you two talk me out of wearing these dumb things?"

Suddenly Jen stopped. She put her arm around Georgie's shoulder. "Look, we don't have to go to that restaurant. It's not so special. Let's get in the car and drive somewhere."

We walked back half a block to where the VW was parked. Georgie sagged into the back seat and kicked off her shoes.

"Aaahh, relief," she sighed.

"We don't even have to go to some stuffy old restaurant. How about a hamburger and fries?" Jen asked. "We could get it at the drive-through and eat on the beach!"

Silence. Ninety-nine percent of the time that would be the perfect suggestion. We'd love it. Love hamburgers, love fries, love eating at the beach.

But not today. Not with our best clothes on; not when

we'd dressed up specially for a fancy restaurant; not when there were gray clouds rolling overhead.

Georgie and Lynn looked at me, question marks on their faces. Georgie shook her head silently, pointing to her dress, her shoes.

"Uh," I stammered. "Well . . ."

But Jen was pulling into the right lane, heading for the hamburger place two blocks away. I could see the big billboard.

"A hamburger sounds good right now. I'm *so* hungry," she said.

I knew Jen liked hamburgers. Doesn't everybody? But usually she liked fancy places even better. The kind of place she'd promised to take us to. The kind we'd dressed up for.

"Hey," I said, trying to sound cheerful and reasonable, "we don't have the right clothes for the beach, Jen. Let's eat them here."

"Don't worry about that," said Jen. "No one will be around to see us."

I groaned inside. That wasn't the point, for Pete's sakes. But looking at that pasted-on smile on her face, I wasn't ready to pull a little-sister act. I wasn't sure *how* to act.

So we drove to Seal Beach. The wide stretch of sand was empty. The sky was gray, the water was green-gray. The sand was damp and cold. It worked itself into my shoes right away, so I yanked them off and tromped through the sand in my best pair of nylons.

Lynn was quiet getting out of the car. She didn't say

much, just threw puzzled glances at Jen. Georgie wasn't so shy.

"Why did she pick *this* place?" she hissed in my ear. "We were supposed to go to a real restaurant. Mom'll kill me if I ruin this skirt."

We didn't have a blanket. There was noplace to put food or to sit or anything. Jen didn't seem to mind. She sat down in the sand as if it was the most ordinary thing in the world to do in a skirt and suit jacket.

"Now isn't this better than a stuffy old restaurant?" she asked. "I just love the beach."

We just stood there, shivering over our cold hamburgers.

"Wow, this is fun." Georgie sulked, but quietly.

"Let's go. Tell Jen we want to go, Robin," Lynn whispered urgently.

"Yeah . . . okay . . ." I dropped down by Jen.

"Jen, we've got our good clothes on. . . ."

But Jen had left her hamburger half-eaten and was mounding the damp sand.

"Sand sculpture," she said, carefully smoothing and shaping. "The sand's perfect today."

"Jen—these are our *good clothes*!"

"Just a sec. I'm going to make a turtle. . . ." I don't think she even heard me.

I stood up; looked over at Georgie and Lynn. Shrugged. What could I do? What could I say?

"We might as well . . . go for a walk. . . ."

"What's wrong with her?' Georgie whispered as soon as

we were out of earshot. "Why is she acting so weird?"

I shrugged again. I was embarrassed, mad, scared.

"Oh, you know how artists are," I said. "They get moody. When Jen gets started on something, she forgets everything else." I tried to sound casual, offhand.

If we'd had the right kind of shoes, we could have gone out on the pier. If the day had been sunny, we might have stopped worrying about nylons getting ruined and about good clothes. We might even have gotten into the spirit of a walk on the beach. I mean, we like the beach, usually.

But the sky was gray and moody, and when we got back to Jen she didn't say anything to us. She just kept working on her sand turtle.

"Jen—" I raised my voice, trying to sound cheery. "That's a . . . nice turtle. Can we go now?"

Jen looked up—and her look made me shiver.

It was the cold-eyed, distant Jen.

"You could at least help me with this," she said. Her voice was cold like her eyes.

My stomach clenched down on the hamburger.

"Uh . . . okay." I knelt beside her, afraid, tense. I didn't want to get this strange Jen mad. I patted at the sand around the turtle's foot, or flipper or whatever it was. Lynn and Georgie stood a few steps away, watching. They didn't complain anymore. They knew something was truly wrong.

It seemed like an hour before Jen was satisfied with that stupid turtle. We walked back to the car in silence. I climbed into the front seat, while Georgie and Lynn huddled together in the back.

Then, all of a sudden Jen got worried about the time. She pulled into the left lane, driving right up to the car ahead of us.

"Hurry up!" she said impatiently, almost driving into the car's bumper. She honked the horn. "Move!"

Georgie and Lynn and I exchanged wide-eyed glances. What was she going to do—drive right into the back window of that car? It was minding its own business and keeping the speed limit.

Jen honked the horn again, then swerved around and passed on the right, almost hitting the car that was coming from behind.

"Jen!" I yelled, grasping the door handle for dear life. "Slow down! You're going too fast! This isn't the freeway!"

"We're late," Jen said angrily. "Have to get home. I spent too long on that damn turtle."

We passed three or four other cars. We got honked at half a dozen times. Any second I expected a cop to come bearing down on us with flashing red lights.

But Jen was lucky. She made it all the way home with no tickets. Just three shook-up kids.

20

MOM KNEW SOMETHING WAS WRONG THE minute we walked in the door. Jen's face, my face; the way Jen walked straight through the living room, with just a bare nod to Mom, the cold distant look—and then right to her bedroom.

"What happened, Robin?" Mom kept asking me, over and over. But I didn't feel like talking much. I was too tight inside.

It was so awful, so embarrassing. Georgie and Lynn were mad. Wrecked shoes, stockings, maybe wrecked clothes. For sure, a wrecked afternoon. They didn't really know what was wrong. They probably thought Jen had acted selfish, moody, weird—but they didn't know why.

"We went to the beach," I said finally. "Jen took us to the *beach*. In these clothes. And she spent hours making a stupid sand turtle."

"I knew I shouldn't have let you go," Mom said. "I *knew* it was a bad idea this week."

Mom thought I was shaky because I'd gotten chilled at the beach. So she made me take a shower. She fixed me soup. And Jen stayed in her room. She didn't come out to eat. She didn't come out when Dad came home. She didn't even talk to her boyfriend when he called her that evening.

So Dad and Gary talked. When Dad got off the phone, he sat down heavily and just stared at the floor for a while.

"We should have talked to Gary before we let Robin go," he said in a low voice to Mom. "He said Jen's been in a strange mood all week. It must be the Lent business again." He shook his head. "Though it sure beats me what Lent has to do with all this. Gary said that Jen really wanted Robin and her friends to come. She wanted to show them a good time." Another weary head shake. "Jen just wasn't up to it."

I heard Mom's sigh all the way from the living room. "It's too bad. Jen was looking forward so much to this shopping trip. . . ."

I knew I was going to cry. I ran to my bedroom and stuffed my face in my pillow so hard I could barely breathe. But that didn't stop the explosion inside me; I was bawling, shaking, flooding the pillow with tears. . . .

I heard a strange sound.

I jerked awake. It was very dark in my room. Had I cried myself to sleep? What time was it? And . . . what was that noise?

It was a voice. Someone was calling—for help.

I sat up in bed. I heard footsteps in the hall, running.

The voice was louder, calling out, crying. It was Jen's voice.

"Give me my knife!"

I started trembling. I reached for the covers to pull them tight around me.

"Jen—" Dad's voice, loud, panicked. "Honey, calm down!"

I had to let go of the covers, had to get up and stumble across the dark room and down the hall.

Dad was trying to hold Jen down. Jen was in bed, writhing, twisting, trying to get up.

"Give me my knife! Give me my knife!"

Horror froze me.

"Help me, Robin," Dad cried, using both hands to pin down Jen's arms.

"Where's Mom," I cried.

"She's on the phone, trying to reach the doctor."

"Dad, get up," Jen begged tearfully. "Please, Dad, why are you *doing* this to me? Get off! Let me up! I want my knife!"

"Jen. Please—"

I ran to the bed. I got on Jen's other side. My hands clamped over her wrist.

I hardly dared to look at her, at my own sister that I was holding down like a criminal or something.

Except it wasn't really her. When she spoke, she knew my name, knew who I was, knew who Dad was. And yet, it was someone else struggling, pleading, crying.

"Let-me-up!" With a great burst of energy she tried to heave herself free. She nearly pulled away from my hands. I got down on all fours, pushing down on her leg with one

hand and her arm with the other, straining to hold one side down while Dad held the other.

"Dad, won't you give me my knife?" It was a girl's voice, not a grown-up voice. "Please won't you just let me have my knife?"

"Honey, I can't. I can't do that, Jen."

"Why are you being so mean? Don't you love me?"

"Oh, honey, you know I do. . . ."

Mom ran in. "I finally reached the doctor. He'll meet us at the hospital. I've called an ambulance."

"Give me my knife!" Another might lunge upward. Dad and I both bore down harder. I knew my fingers were making red marks on Jen's wrist, knew it must hurt when I pushed down so hard.

"Please, Robin." She turned to me. "Robin, get my knife for me. *Please.*"

I shook my head and looked away, swallowing the huge lump in my throat.

"Damn it! I want my knife!"

The ambulance came quickly, quietly. No sirens. The men carried Jen, still struggling, out of the house. They took her to the hospital.

21

JEN WAS IN THAT HOSPITAL FOR A WEEK.
Then she was moved to a private hospital. She stayed there
over a month. After the first few weeks, Mom and Dad let
me come with them for a visit.

On the outside, the hospital looked nice. Pretty, green
lawns, flower beds, big avocado trees. There was a nice
lobby, too, with bright furniture. Still, my stomach felt
tight, jumpy. Would this place be full of weird people?
Would Jen be locked in some room? Would she be . . .
okay?

Then I saw her walking down the hall toward the lobby.
She was wearing a pretty blouse and matching capri pants;
her hair was brushed nicely. She was smiling.

"Robin!" Her hug was tight, fierce. "Oh, I'm so glad to
see you!"

"Me, too!" I hugged her back, tightly. A wonderful
warm, happy feeling poured through me. Jen was herself.
Her wonderful, pretty self.

"I'll show you around this place," Jen said to me, her arm
around my shoulder. She led us down the hall. Her room

looked like a regular old hospital room. No big bars or locks. I didn't see any weird-looking people, either.

Jen was happy, cheerful. She even joked. "When I first came here, they didn't give me knives with my place setting," she said, with a rueful sort of smile.

"I wonder why," Mom said wryly. And with those few words, the whole nightmare suddenly stopped being a dark, awful, unnamed scene in my mind. It became something you could talk about in the open, even sort of joke about.

Anyway, Jen looked okay now. Really okay. Even a little tan. She probably had lots of time to sit in the sun. I mean, what was there to *do* at a place like this? Watch TV? Talk to doctors?

Jen gave me an especially hard hug when it was time to go. "You and me, we have some catching up to do," she whispered. For the first time there was a little tremble in her voice. Her arms tightened, as though she didn't want to let me go. "We'll make up for lost time when I come home, okay?"

"You bet," I whispered over the sudden scratchy, lumpy feeling in the back of my throat.

I didn't want to go. Still, the visit had been good. Mom and Dad were more relaxed. This was an okay hospital. There were pretty flower beds, and cheery-looking people in uniforms all over the place.

Surely, with all those nurses and doctors, by now *somebody* had figured out what was wrong with Jen and had given it a name. I wanted to know what. I *needed* to know.

I leaned forward in the back seat.

"Mom, is there a name for what's wrong with Jen?" I blurted out.

Mom glanced at Dad, then back at me. She took a breath. I could almost see her arguing with herself in her head. Then in a slow, careful, almost soothing voice, she said, "It's a type of . . . sickness, you see. And it makes Jen act . . . not like herself—"

"I know, I know. But what *is* it?"

Mom glanced over at Dad again. She looked back at me, fiddled with the ring on her finger. "Robin, I don't really know . . . how to explain it. As I said, Jen has times when she acts like . . . someone else. Like a little girl. Or like a . . . stranger." Her voice wasn't so calm anymore. It was tight, clipped. She didn't want to be telling me this. "Like she has . . ."

"Split personality," Dad said grimly.

I looked from him to Mom.

"What?" I said. "What's that?"

Mom sighed. "As I said, it's acting like someone else. Like a different person."

"What? I don't get it." My voice sounded shrill. I thought of the cold-eyed Jen, on the beach; Jen crying like a little girl for a knife.

"I don't *get* it," I said again, desperately. My fingers curled around the window handle, squeezing it hard. Other people had times when they acted mad or like a baby or cried, but it wasn't the same. It wasn't like . . . *this*.

"No one does," Mom said wearily. Then she turned and

put her hand on my shoulder. "Robin, Jen doesn't even know when it happens. She doesn't remember when she's acted like that. It's nothing she does on purpose."

I thought back to that day Jen came in the ugly red dress. And how she hadn't remembered it later. How could you forget something like that?

"But . . ." My mind was whirling. I didn't understand.

"Her doctor's helping her. He's trying to find out if anything happened when she was little to make . . . this happen."

Was that what that stuff, that Sodium Pentothal, was for?

Mom's fingers dug into my shoulder. "Now, you are not to worry and stew about this, Robin." Her tone was firm again. Her eyes locked with mine. "Our job is to be there for Jen. And she is better. You can see that. Things will work out."

I did not worry and stew about it. I did not even *think* about it. I thought instead about Jen the way she was today. The *real* Jen, the one who was getting better, who would not act weird anymore. I turned up my little transistor radio in the back seat, even though the reception was lousy, and I played staticky music the rest of the trip home. For once, Mom and Dad didn't yell at me to shut it off. At home I kept on playing it, loud, in my bedroom, until they finally did tell me to turn it down. Then I stomped outside and walked around the yard and ended up at my shrine.

I don't know why I went there. I hadn't been back to the old club-spot for such a long time. I'd sort of forgotten about the shrine lately.

The Hula Hoop wasn't standing like a big halo altar around the statue of Our Lady anymore. It had fallen over and was lying in the weeds, crusted with dried mud. The statue was hidden in the tall weeds. Not much was left to make it look like a shrine or sacred place.

Had that dirty Hula Hoop really *glowed* once? Had it really been a bright and shining ring of light hanging in midair? That night when I thought I saw it had been a crazy awful night. I'd been sort of fasting and was so hungry I was half-dizzy. I'd been real upset. When you're dizzy and crying, you can imagine all sorts of things. Even, maybe, a vision.

Standing there in the twilight, I shut my eyes and tried, desperately, to bring it back: the image of the glowing hoop; the breathless, tingly, holy feeling that anything was possible—that miracles hovered, unseen, ready to touch down . . .

But I couldn't feel anything except disbelief.

22

JEN AND I DIDN'T GET A CHANCE TO CATCH UP
again until the middle of summer, the day of the house-
warming party at Jen's new apartment. A pool party! And
Georgie and Lynn were invited.

"You won't believe what I'm wearing under my
clothes," Lynn whispered, squeezed between Georgie and
me in the back seat of our car. "A bikini!" Her face got pink
just from her saying the word. She shot an embarrassed look
toward Mom and Dad in the front seat.

"A *bikini!*" Georgie yelped.

"Shut up!" Lynn clapped her hand over Georgie's
mouth. "Do you want everyone on the whole freeway to
hear?"

"Let's see!" I poked her.

She got red again. "Not *here.*" She bit her lip. "I just can't
believe I really bought it. I can't believe I'm wearing it. I
just saw it there on the sale table, and I tried it on just for
fun and . . . and then I bought it." Her voice was full of
wonder.

"Itsy-bitsy-teeny-weeny-yellow-polka-dot-bikini!" Georgie and I started singing at the top of our lungs. Lynn

tried to clap her hands over both our mouths and ended up falling into my lap.

"No!" Lynn howled, mortified. "Don't tell everyone! I'm going to *die*!"

"Better not die now," Dad said, pulling into the parking lot. "We're here."

"You're going to love Jen and Linda's new place." Mom gathered up the beach bag stuffed with our towels and suntan lotion. "The girls have fixed it up real cute."

Mom sounded happy enough about Jen's apartment now. But she hadn't liked the idea at all in the beginning. She and Dad had both wanted Jen to live at home over the summer. There'd been a lot of phone calls and arguments. Mom and Dad had finally given in when Jen's doctor okayed the plan.

I was so glad Jen had asked me to invite Lynn and Georgie, and so glad they wanted to come. Perhaps they'd forgotten all about that strange day at the beach. Maybe it hadn't been a big deal for them. Maybe they'd believed me that all artists acted crazy sometimes.

"Who else is coming to this party?" Lynn asked nervously, trying to stretch her T-shirt to pull it farther down over her bikini.

"Jen's boyfriend and some other college friends." I climbed out of the car.

"They're celebrating Jen's finishing her makeup work from when . . . she was sick." Mom's voice sort of drifted off with the last few words. Then she smiled. "You know Jen—any excuse for a party."

"Hey, Linda, they're here!" There was Jen now, waving at us from the sidewalk, a white shirt hanging loosely over her blue bathing suit.

I ran toward her. "You're so *tan*. I hate you!" I hugged her hard. I hadn't seen Jen since that visit at the hospital in the spring. She'd been busy with her makeup college work and with moving. I hugged her tighter. "I want a tan like that!"

"I don't think I'm going to swim after all," Lynn muttered miserably. "My tan is from my other suit. I don't think I'll even take off my shirt. Why did I buy this bikini?" she moaned.

"You'll swim," I said knowingly. It was so hot today, nobody in his right mind could stay out of that cool-looking blue water.

"Come on, Lynn, time to show all!" Georgie started toward Lynn, smiling wickedly. "We want to see your itsy-bitsy-teeny-weeny—"

"*No!*" Lynn yelled, clutching her arms together tightly across her middle and backing away. "Get away from me. Help!" she screamed as we both came toward her. "*Help!*" she hollered again, giggling and mad at the same time. "Help, somebody! Robin and Georgie are trying to strip me!"

Georgie grabbed one arm and I grabbed the other.

"Help!" Lynn looked around desperately, then yanked away from us, held her nose, and jumped into the pool, T-shirt and all.

"Now see what you made me do!" She came up, choking, giggling, flailing her arms. "You made me get my shirt wet!"

She swam all afternoon with her big T-shirt stuck to her, soggy and wet, while we all played water polo, tried goofy dives, and gathered around the patio, where the picnic tables and barbecue were set up.

Georgie poked me as she went by with her plate. "These college guys are really cute," she whispered. Then, to Lynn, "If I had a bikini, I'd sure wear it."

"I bet you would," Lynn said, wringing out the bottom of her drenched T-shirt. I didn't tell her that with her T-shirt clinging to her, everyone could pretty much tell what her bikini looked like, anyway.

"*These* college guys are all taken," I informed Georgie. "And they hardly know we're here, besides."

It was true. Except for the water-polo game, they'd spent the whole party sitting around the patio, yakking about college stuff—tests, paper, grades—the way they were doing right now.

"Hey, Jen, what did you get on that makeup paper you did on 'Time'?" Linda called out.

"B-plus," Jen answered, putting out more dip. "Should have been an A, for all the work I put into it."

"So what did you finally decide about time travel?" Gary scooped a potato chip into the dip and held it out to Jen, laughing. "Are we all going to be traveling through time in the future?"

"No, I don't think so," Jen said. She chewed the potato chip thoughtfully. "I did a lot of thinking about it for this paper, and this is what I decided: If someone in the future invents some time machine, then people from the future would use it to travel back into our time, or some other time, wouldn't they? So, how come not one time traveler has been discovered yet? Wouldn't you think at least *one* would have been found—if it's going to happen?"

"Huh?" asked Linda. "The future hasn't happened yet, remember?"

"But time is *one*," Jen argued. "So the idea of time travel seems possible, only like I said, no one from the future seems to be doing it."

Linda shook her head. "I'm afraid this conversation is too deep for me." She turned to Gary. "How does it feel to be going with someone with a genius IQ?"

Gary smiled and put his arm around Jen. "Well," he drawled, "all I can say is: Takes one to know one."

Jen rolled her eyes. "You used to be conceited, but now you're perfect, right? That's enough about school! Turn up the radio, someone. Let's dance!"

The first song was a twist.

Lynn and Georgie and I danced with one another. Then the record changed to "Rock around the Clock" and Jen and Gary and their friends started bopping.

"I wish I could do that," Lynn said wistfully, watching them shuffle and spin all over the patio.

"We tried to learn in gym," Georgie said. "Only when

my partner swung me, our hands slipped and I spun right into the wall." She scowled. "Creep. I bet he did it on purpose."

Lynn pulled her knees up to her chin, shivering a little. "Jen and Gary are the best dancers." She sighed. "Robin, they're such a handsome, perfect couple!"

She was right. Jen and Gary were swinging and whirling, faster, faster, faster. When the song ended, Jen sort of dance-jumped right into Gary's arms, and he caught her. "Tah-dah!" Jen flung out her arms.

Everyone clapped. Jen and Gary bowed. "Thank you, thank you." Jen laughed and reached for her beer on the table. "Wow, I'm out of shape," she panted.

"Where did she learn all those fancy steps?" Georgie cried enviously. "Can you talk her into teaching us? Oh, Robin, this is the greatest party! I hope it keeps going all night!"

But three or four songs later, I could see Mom walking around starting to collect towels. "Girls, you'd better go change into dry clothes now," she called out. "It's a long drive home. We'll have to get going."

"I just brought a beach jacket," Georgie said.

"And I'm wearing my clothes," Lynn looked up sheepishly, tugging her T-shirt down.

I grabbed my bag of clothes. "Be right back. I'll change in Jen's room." I half danced across the patio, to the tune of "Purple People Eater" blaring from the radio, and skipped into the apartment.

I stopped in the bedroom doorway.

Jen was sitting cross-legged on her bed, leaning against the headboard, hugging her teddy bear, Rupert. Just sitting there, squeezing him, rocking a little, making small sounds . . .

I froze. My hand gripped the doorjamb hard.

She looked up and smiled a big open smile. "Hi, Robin," she said in a singsong voice.

The apartment was warm, but I started to shiver violently in my wet suit.

She was supposed to be all right. She was supposed to be all right. She was *supposed* to be all right!

"No," I breathed. "No, no, *no*." I turned and fled down the hall, practically knocking Mom down.

"Mom," I cried, grabbing her. "Mom—" I pointed to Jen's room. "Jen—"

"I know," she said. "Dad just told me." She looked old, there in the hall.

She took me by the shoulders, steering me back down the hall. "Time to go, Robin. The party's over."

"But Mom, I thought—"

"I'm going to stay here. Dad will take you girls home."

"But Mom." She wasn't letting me finish. "I thought they cured her in that hospital. I thought she wasn't sick anymore."

"It's not that easy, Robin. It takes time," Mom said wearily. "I think, tonight . . . it was the beer. I think . . . she'll be okay . . . in the morning."

All the way home in the car, while Georgie slept, leaning on one side of me, and Lynn slept, leaning on the other side,

I tried to forget how it'd looked—Jen in the bedroom with the teddy bear, that friendly little-kid smile on her face. But the awful scene wouldn't go away. It stayed there, like a big poster slapped against my brain.

When we got home, the first thing I saw when I walked into my bedroom was Jen's picture of the little girl, up on the wall. Jen's little girl. Jen—little girl. Little, sad girl. Little girl, little girl . . .

She was supposed to be better!

I turned away from the mocking picture. I wrapped my arms around my knees and stared out my window into the summer darkness.

Somewhere out there, my shrine was hiding in the dark and the weeds.

She was supposed to be better!

If doctors couldn't cure her, and if . . .

Well, was this miracle business like Santa Claus and the tooth fairy? Believe it till you get old enough to know better? It couldn't be. There were all those proven miracles in the history books. Over and over again, down through history: blind men seeing, lame men walking, all that stuff. At all those other shrines.

My eyes probed the night desperately, for a light, a sign. . . .

There was no moon. Only a hazy darkness that covered the whole yard, and the sticky-sweet smell of jasmine.

I couldn't see a thing.

In the Park

That was the night of my un-vision. I have now walked most of the way across the park with my Hula Hoop. I'm not rolling it now, just bumping it along. It's wet and cold, and my hands are wet and cold, but I feel better. Walking helps. The cold air helps. Thinking about *then* instead of *now* helps.

But the memories are getting very close. Eighth grade next. Sister Teresa for a teacher. The time of the late-night calls . . . when I was supposed to be asleep and I found out the secrets I wasn't supposed to know.

Part 4
Eighth Grade

23

"YOU WON'T BELIEVE WHAT SISTER TERESA does!" I slammed my notebook down on Lynn's couch, and kicked off my shoes. "She gives these stupid oral quizzes. She asks you a question, and if you don't know the answer, you have to stay standing—even though we're in the eighth grade. You can't sit down until someone else misses a question. And I was the first one it happened to. It was *awful*! Everyone stares at you! I thought I was going to die!"

"You have to stand up to answer questions?" Lynn looked at me incredulously. "We never stand up to answer questions at my school. You should go to public school."

I leaned back against the couch, eyes shut, reliving the torture, the humiliation. " 'What's the capital of Yugoslavia?' she asks me. I don't know the capital of Yugoslavia. Who cares about the capital of Yugoslavia? And so I had to stand there, just stand there, with all the boys staring at me, until somebody else missed a question." I shuddered, thinking about it. "I hate eighth grade! I'll never make it through a whole year of this. And tomorrow she's doing it again. A pop quiz on rocks." I waved my science book at her.

"I'm glad I go to public school," Lynn said fervently. "They don't torture us like that at all. And I love Home Ec. We're doing fabric and colors now. Hey, Robin." She bounced in her chair. "Let's do my bedroom!"

I stared past the living room into the mess that was her bedroom. Hers and her twin sisters'. The bratlets. There were two sets of bunk beds that took up all the wall space, and there was a little bit of space left in the middle of the floor. It was heaped with dirty clothes and toys. Lynn's all-time favorite game was planning how to redo it into a magazine dream room.

She leaned back with a faraway look on her face. "How about . . . peach this time? We haven't tried that yet. Wouldn't that be a great color for a bedroom? Peach curtains, bedspread, *one* bed. And a ruffled peach skirt on the vanity. And a fluffy peach rug . . ."

"Too much peach," I said. We'd planned her room in just about every color scheme imaginable: pink and white, lavender and white, lavender and pink, yellow and orange, blue and green, even black and red. Once we'd tried to do it for real. We raided her mom's linen closet and draped yellow sheets all over everything, even over the dirty clothes on the floor. Then we re-covered all the books on her bookshelf with aluminum foil for a sparkly finishing touch. Her mom just about hit the ceiling when she saw it. Another time we made floor plans of her redecorated room, with attached bathroom, and patio doors leading out to a sunken pool.

". . . or maybe . . . how about peach and aqua? How about

that, Robin? Aqua rug, peach bedspread, and aqua canopy!"

"Yoo-hoo!" Georgie's voice called. "I'm here." Georgie breezed in to join our homework sessions every now and then, but she usually left her book closed in her lap while she brushed her hair.

Today she didn't even have homework along. "Hey, guys," she said, plopping into the armchair. "I just got the greatest idea! Let's have a Halloween party at one of our houses, and now that we're on the subject, let's invite boys!"

"Whose house?" Lynn asked. "My mom wouldn't let me."

"Neither would mine," I muttered, staring at the millions of rocks I'd have to read about and know before tomorrow.

"Come on, you could talk your mom into it, couldn't you, Lynn?" Georgie turned to her first. "Wouldn't it be great? Bobbing for apples, with *boys*!"

"There's no place for any kind of party in this crummy house," Lynn said, waving her arm toward the cramped bedroom, skinny kitchen, cluttered living room. "The only place you could bob for apples is the bathtub. I'd die before I'd invite a bunch of kids here."

"Well then, how about you, Robin?" Georgie swung toward me.

"Can't," I said again, irritably. Stupid Georgie. Why didn't she and Lynn have ten thousand rocks to memorize? Why didn't she and Lynn have to worry about standing in embarrassment and feeling like a ten-foot Amazon if they missed one stupid question? How come all she had to worry about was Halloween parties?

"My mom said I can't have a party with boys until I'm fourteen," I lied. I threw my book down. "And I'll never ever learn all these stupid rocks before tomorrow!" I glared at Georgie, Lynn, the living room, the world.

"My, my. Mustn't get violent." Georgie giggled. "I was just asking. Can't blame a person for that." She rolled her eyes. "Touchy, touchy."

I ignored her and grabbed up my books. Let her giggle. Let her plan her stupid parties. I wasn't going to be the one standing up in Sister Teresa's classroom tomorrow. I was going to learn those rocks if I had to stay up all night.

And not just that night. For weeks I studied my books inside out, upside down, and backward. Every fact about the Revolutionary War, the geography of Europe, the life cycle of the tsetse fly, the names of the popes, the names of the presidents. I studied late. I tossed and turned at bedtime, counting capitals and mountain ranges.

That's how I heard the late-night phone calls.

The first one was about eleven o'clock of the day Georgie brought up the party idea. Mom answered it in the kitchen. Her voice was low because it was late. But by lying perfectly still, hardly breathing, I could hear most of it.

"Jen? What? Oh, honey, I've already told you everything I can . . ."

Silence.

"All right, go ahead."

Another silence. A long one. When Mom spoke again,

she didn't sound a bit sleepy or groggy anymore. Her voice trembled a bit.

"Jen, I didn't know him that well. I mostly talked to his wife, Dorothy, when I picked you up. I do know that he got very sick, with cancer . . . but it was so long ago—"

Another long silence. Then Mom must have walked with the phone to the table. Her voice got farther away, muffled. I couldn't make sense of the whispers.

I lay in the dark, staring at the ceiling. Who was very sick? Why did Mom sound so upset? What had happened long ago?

24

"I BEGGED AND *BEGGED*," GEORGIE SAID IN disgust the next afternoon, pulling weed strands apart with her fingers. "I told them, 'Look, I'll be fourteen in a few months. I'm old enough to have a party, for Pete's sakes!' So"—she ripped off another segment—"they finally said I could invite you two for supper and they'd take us to the drive-in movie." She plopped back against the fence with a sigh. "Not exactly the kind of party I had in mind—boys . . . dancing . . . music . . ."

I nudged Lynn. "Maybe we should both get crew cuts and wear slacks. Maybe then she'd like us to come to her party."

"You know what I mean." Georgie sighed again. "It would have been so much fun. We could have used the garage and danced in there . . . oh well, I guess this will be better than nothing."

"Thanks a lot," Lynn said. "We love you, too."

I bowed. "Humble servant much honored at invitation."

Actually, it was an honor. Georgie's parents were always so busy with their restaurant, they were hardly ever home. She must have worked pretty hard on her parents if they really were letting her officially invite us for dinner.

"The drive-in will be fun, anyway." Georgie started on another weed strand. "It's bargain night. Three features for the price of two. And if the movies aren't any good, we can eat popcorn and watch the people in the other cars."

When Lynn and I arrived at Georgie's for the big night, the kitchen table was set for just the three of us, with a white linen tablecloth, pretty blue china plates, and a vase of flowers in the middle. You sure could tell that they were restaurant people; each place had a glass of ice water and . . . a glass of tomato juice.

"Hello, girls," Mrs. Nelson said, frying pork chops at the stove. "We'll have you eat right away so we can get going to the movies!" She gave us a big cheery smile.

It was an order. Sit down and eat.

We sat down. Lynn rolled her eyes at me, pointing to the glass of tomato juice.

"Do we have to drink this?" she mouthed to Georgie.

Georgie's eyes went to her mom, then back to the full glasses. She made a face, nodding silently.

They weren't even the small glasses that tomato juice usually came in. They were the big, tall kind of glasses that sane people put milk in. Or lemonade. Or pop. Poor Georgie. Did she have to drink tomato juice every day?

Georgie's mom set a platter of pork chops in front of us, with a piece of parsley in the middle. "Help yourselves and eat up," she said with a big smile. "With three features to watch, we'll be there half the night."

"Sounds great," I said politely, my eyes still on the tomato juice.

What if I left it? What could she do to me? Never invite me over again? She probably wouldn't anyway.

But there was something about Georgie's mom—even when she was smiling and cheery like she was now—that made you *know* you'd just better behave. Underneath that smile was pure steel. I'd heard her yell at Georgie a few times. Well, a glass of tomato juice wouldn't exactly kill me.

Lynn was the bravest. She picked up her glass and took a big gulp, then shoved in a forkful of pork chop.

"Lynn, how are those cute twin sisters of yours?" asked Mrs. Nelson, setting out the potatoes. "I see them playing in the yard every day when I go to work. What are their names again?"

"Carrie and Connie." Lynn swallowed hard, turning to face Georgie's mom. Quick as a flash, Georgie reached over and dumped some of her own tomato juice into Lynn's glass.

Lynn's eyes got huge when she saw her glass, full to the very brim. She knew right away who had done it. "You rat," she hissed across the table to Georgie. She lifted her glass. For a second I thought she was going to throw it at Georgie, she looked so mad. But instead she took a deep breath and downed another gulp.

Georgie's mom came toward us with the applesauce. "You girls did tell your parents you'd be getting back really late, didn't you?"

"Yes," I said, reaching to take the bowl from her. When I turned back to the table, my tomato juice glass was filled almost to overflowing. A tiny red trickle ran down the outside edge. Georgie's glass was half-full.

"Georgie!" I kicked her under the table.

"Hey!" Her eyes were wide, innocent. "Robin, such manners." Then she grinned wickedly. "Drink your juice, so we can get going."

"We'll be leaving in about twenty minutes." Georgie's mom hurried to answer the phone ringing at the other side of the kitchen.

I kicked Georgie again, hard.

"You *rat*," I copied Lynn's words. "Dumping your stupid tomato juice on *us.*"

"Yeah!" Lynn's cheeks looked like they'd been dipped in the stuff, they were so red. She picked up her glass and held it in front of Georgie. "I can't drink any more of this awful stuff!"

"Me neither!"

"Shhh." Georgie's eyes went to her mom talking on the phone. "We have to do something with it." She looked around desperately. "I know—the flowers!"

"What?"

Georgie glanced at her mom again. Still on the phone. She grabbed the vase in the center of the table. "Pour the tomato juice in here," she whispered. "Hurry!'

"But it's already full of water!"

"Wait a sec . . ." She picked up the vase and tipped it sideways, so that the water poured into her water glass. A slimy piece of stem poured out with it, wrapping around the edge of her glass. The water was slightly green. It smelled.

"Yuck!"

"Shhh . . . now, quick! Pour in the tomato juice!"

A good thing it was a wide-mouthed vase. It held all of my juice and all of Lynn's. But red stuff started oozing out of the top of the vase before Georgie got all of hers dumped in.

"It's too full. Stop!"

"What am I going to do with the rest of this slop?" Georgie stared at her glass. Lynn and I both clutched our empty glasses, to keep them that way.

"I know." Georgie started digging a hole in her mound of mashed potatoes. Carefully she poured the rest of her tomato juice in the hole, turning it into a red swimming pool, then covered it with more mashed potatoes.

Lynn and I watched, fascinated, as she spooned some into her mouth. "Not bad," she mumbled. "Sort of like ketchup and mashed potatoes."

"Mashed potatoes and tomato juice," Lynn whispered in disbelief.

I stared at the big white hill of mashed potatoes, with little red rivers running down it like lava. "Volcano," I giggled. "Eruption of Mount Mashed Potatoes!"

"No." Lynn tried to make her voice low and dramatic, but the giggle came out and ruined the effect. "It's *bleeding*. All over the place. B–Burst artery!"

"Attack of the red slime!"

"Cavern of the bubbling blood!"

Georgie clapped her hand over her mouth to keep the mashed potatoes in, through the giggles, but some spattered out anyway. "Stop," she gasped, spitting more mashed potatoes across the table.

"Robin . . . they're on your plate." Lynn pointed to the telltale spattering of potatoes. "Attack!" She held up her napkin as a shield.

"Georgina Nelson!" Her mom had hung up the phone. She stared at the three of us across the kitchen. "What is going on here!"

"S-Sorry," Georgie gasped. Her eyes were bulging. She leaned way back, trying to control herself. And fell on the floor.

That did it. Lynn and I got up and ran out of the kitchen and into the bathroom. We stuffed towels in our mouths and shook helplessly, while out in the kitchen Georgie's mom's voice went on and on angrily.

". . . disgraceful! Spitting food across the table! Look at that tablecloth . . . thoroughly ashamed . . . !"

Half an hour later she was still mad, driving us across town to pick up Georgie's dad at the restaurant. I knew she would have gladly taken Lynn and me home and forgotten the whole rest of the party. But she went ahead and drove us to the drive-in. The three of us sat straight and stiff in the back seat.

At least Georgie's dad was in a good mood.

"Haven't seen a Jerry Lewis movie in ages," he said as the movie started.

"Mom likes Jerry Lewis, too," Georgie whispered. "As soon as he starts cracking jokes, she'll get in a good mood again, I'll bet."

Sure enough, before long, Mr. and Mrs. Nelson were both laughing their heads off in the front seat. Georgie and Lynn and I kept busy watching the other cars.

"Look over there," Lynn poked me. "Look at those two in the back seat!"

Georgie leaned out the window, gaping. "*Wow.* Would you look at *that.* Oops. Going D-O-W-N. Can't see them anymore." She giggled. "Wonder where they disappeared to."

Mrs. Nelson turned around to glare at us. "Will you girls please keep your voices down and watch the movie?" she said in a voice that could have frozen tomato juice.

"Yes, ma'am." Georgie shrunk down in her seat.

The second feature was an old Dracula movie. Every time a bloody victim showed up on the huge screen, Georgie elbowed me and whispered, "Tomato juice!"

But by the beginning of the third show, my eyes were feeling gritty and it was hard to concentrate.

The movie didn't even look interesting. No monsters or murderers. Just some washed-out-looking lady named Eve.

I slid back against the door and yawned. Lynn's eyes were closed. Georgie was still watching the other cars, but in a half-asleep sort of way.

"Isn't it bizarre?" Georgie's mom said in the front seat. "Split personality. Do you think it can really happen like that?"

"It's supposed to be a true story, isn't it?" Mr. Nelson yawned.

I sat up straight and stared at the huge screen. Split personality? Had Georgie's mom really said that? The same words my mom had used that day when I asked about Jen? I started watching the screen.

The woman named Eve wasn't so mousy-looking now. She was wearing a slinky cocktail dress and acting like a whole different, sexy person. "I'm Eve Black," she was telling the doctor. "Not Eve White."

The sleepy feeling was completely gone. While Georgie nodded on one side of me and Lynn softly snored on the other, I watched the whole movie. Watched while this lady, Eve, changed back and forth between the quiet Eve White and the sexy Eve Black and then turned into somebody else named Jane. Split personality. Three people living inside one person.

The day Mom and Dad had tried to explain it to me, they'd said Jen acted like "someone else." I hadn't understood.

Now, watching the movie, I did. It wasn't just "acting" like someone else. It was "being" someone else.

Now I knew what split personality meant.

I'd laughed through the Dracula movie and giggled about the blood and tomato juice. But this movie, *The Three Faces of Eve,* was the real horror movie. This one brought goose bumps to my arms. Because they could have made a movie just like this and called it *The Three Faces of Jen.*

Something had happened to that Eve when she was little, to make her like that.

Was that why Jen needed the Sodium Pentothal? She told Dad it would help her remember back to when she was real little. Was that to find out if something bad happened to *her,* too?

25

THE NEXT LATE-NIGHT CALL WAS ABOUT SIX weeks later. By that time just about everyone in our class had taken their turn at missing questions and standing like a dunce: the smartest kids, the most popular kids, everyone. It was still torture, but it was shared torture. I wasn't feeling so worried about it. I wasn't staying up so late, studying in bed. So when the phone rang, I was asleep. I had to fight my way back up through layers of drowsiness. The first part of the conversation drifted above me in a sleep haze.

". . . they baby-sat you every day while I worked. They were wonderful people . . . lived a block away . . ."

Silence.

"Well, I don't know. Let me think. You were three . . . no, about four. Yes. Four years old. They thought the world of you, especially Les. But he was so sick . . . he died that same year."

I was wide awake now. Was "he" the same "he" of the last phone call? The baby-sitter?

Silence. A long, long silence. When Mom spoke again, her voice really shook. "Jen, it's so . . . hard for me to

. . . hear this. He was such a wonderful man. He never would have done . . ."

Silence.

"Yes, the brain tumor did change him, but still, honey, he wouldn't ever have done anything like—"

Silence.

"Jen." Mom could hardly talk. "It's not that I don't believe you. Listen, no, Jen. I just can't . . . yes, honey, in the morning. All right?"

Footsteps in the hall. Dad's. I heard the phone click down. And Dad's voice. He wasn't trying to be quiet.

"It's that Sodium Pentothal business again, isn't it? That truth serum."

"Shhh, keep your voice down. Robin's asleep."

"So what is she telling you now? The same story?"

They were walking toward their bedroom. Their voices grew fainter. The door shut.

26

IN THE MORNING, WHEN I FIRST WOKE UP, I thought I'd dreamed the phone call. But the memory didn't fade the way dreams usually do. In the sunny bedroom there was a darkness—a darkness that had no name. A darkness from long ago. It had to do with somebody named Les, who had died a long time before I was born. It was something bad. Something bad that had happened to Jen, when she was a little girl.

Again my eyes went to the picture of the sad little girl. There was something about that picture—the expression on her face, the way she stared off into the distance . . . so unhappy.

Did Jen paint that because *she* had been sad when she was little? Because of . . . something bad that had happened? Little suspicions coiled like snakes in my head. Suspicions with the smell of something wrong, dark, evil.

I thought again about that movie. Something bad happened to Eve when she was a little girl, too.

The darkness followed me like a shadow through the day. It was hard to concentrate at school. Luckily Sister Teresa called on everyone else but me. First, Mike Wilson missed the question about where the Pyrenees Mountains were. Denise Whitman didn't know who Alexander Hamilton was. Then Linda Peters said that the way to find the circumference of a circle was to add up all the sides. So many kids were popping up and down, it was like a room full of jack-in-the-boxes.

It put Sister in a bad mood. "It is obvious that people in this class are not doing their homework," she declared in her iciest, sternest voice. "So, boys and girls, this afternoon we will do some extra work. I want a two-page report from each one of you on some topic from your church-history book."

There were groans and moans all over the class.

"I'm going to do the Crusades," Bobby McElroy whispered behind me. "I did a report on them last year, and I still remember some of the stuff. It'll be a cinch."

"Good idea," I whispered back. I tried to think. Was there anything I'd already done a report on that I could use again?

The thing I'd been the most interested in last year was . . . miracles. Yeah. I'd paid the most attention when we'd come to pictures of shrines and stories of miracles. Because of my Hula Hoop shrine. Well, that'd be as good a topic as any. Maybe I'd find out if miracles really were like Santa Claus and the tooth fairy, if I did the research.

I checked the index of my book. Wow. There were dozens of pages that had the word *miracle*—practically every other page in the book! This was going to take a while.

I started leafing through. Some pages just mentioned the word in passing. Others had whole paragraphs about miracles like the ones in the days of the apostles and early saints. They had miracles all over the place. Later on, in the Middle Ages, huge, fancy churches were built over the places where the miracles had happened.

I looked at the pictures of some of those fancy churches that took hundreds of people years and years to build, and I thought of the puny little "shrine" I'd made in the backyard, at the end of sixth grade. So stupid. So childish.

Things were clear to me now. Sister Agnes Joseph had been right. There really were miracles, but they happened back in those long-ago holy times when saints were walking around and people were building those cathedrals all over the place. I jotted down some sentences about the miracles I'd read about in the textbook. Then I scribbled out a quick ending sentence to my report: "Miracles mostly happened hundreds of years ago. People are not holy enough anymore." And I turned in my report.

When I got home I went back behind the garage and picked up the statue of Our Lady and cleaned her off in the sink. I set her on my bedroom shelf. It was probably a sacrilege or something to leave her out in the rain and mud and all.

But the Hula Hoop was so dirty. Even if I cleaned it off, where would I put it?

I left it lying there in the weeds.

27

IT WAS GETTING NEAR CHRISTMAS AGAIN.

"I talked to Jen at lunch today," Mom said when she got home from work. "She's decided not to go to Big Bear with her college friends for Christmas break after all." She paused. "She and Gary are thinking about . . . splitting up."

I looked up in horror. "Splitting up! But they're *perfect* together!"

"Now, it's not definite," Mom said quickly. "They just need some time apart, to sort things out."

"And no wonder." Dad shook his head. "It hasn't exactly been a bed of roses for the two of them."

Mom took a deep breath. "So—Jen's spending the holidays with us," she said, her tone suddenly a bit too cheerful. "It'll be nice to have her here for Christmas. Jen loves to help with the decorating and baking. Won't it be fun, Robin?"

"Yeah," I said, hoping it would be fun. Wanting it to be. But if Jen was sad about Gary, would she change to . . . the cold Jen, or the little girl?

I didn't want her to come like that.

I did not want that.

But I needn't have worried. Jen wasn't depressed at all; she pulled into the driveway in her VW, honked a hello, and breezed in with her suitcase.

"Well, here I am, home for the holidays!" she announced to Mom and Dad. Mom gave her a big hug.

I think Mom and Dad had probably expected Jen to be moody, and sad, too. They'd probably been worried about the visit, like I'd been.

I felt as if a big weight had floated off me. Jen unpacked her suitcase and set some of her things around the room. She hung up her clothes and turned on the radio. Pop music, but soft.

She set her teddy bear on the bed.

"Old Rupert," she said fondly, patting his mangy fur. "Rupert and I have been together for so long."

After dinner, Jen and I made a cinnamon coffee cake.

"You do the dry ingredients; I'll do the wet ones," Jen directed, rolling up her sleeves, dumping in shortening and sugar. "Don't forget to sift." She started stirring hard with the wooden spoon. "Won't a coffee cake taste good for breakfast instead of cornflakes?"

I checked the recipe. "For the filling we need one cup brown sugar and—"

"No, don't follow the recipe." Jen shook her head. "Cinnamon filling is *so* yummy. Double it. No. *Triple* it.

"Triple it!"

"Yeah. What the hell." Jen grinned. "I mean, if you're going to make a cinnamon coffee cake, then you should *really* fill it with cinnamon!"

"Yeah." I grinned back, dumping in the whole cannister of brown sugar. "What the hell." I liked the reckless sound of that. "What the hell," I said again, reaching for the walnuts.

Jen raised her eyebrows. "Mom wouldn't like to hear you say that, you know."

"What the hell," I answered back, and then we both laughed.

I woke up early the next morning. The rest of the house was completely quiet. But I wasn't the only one awake. When I tiptoed down the hall toward the bathroom, I saw Jen's door half open and a light on inside her room. I poked my head in.

Jen was sitting on her bed, writing in a notebook.

"Hey," I said softly.

She looked up. "Robin! You're up early."

"So are you." I slipped into the room. "What are you doing?" Then I noticed the notebook. It was the one with the purple cover. "Are you writing stories?"

"Not exactly." Jen gave me a thoughtful look, as if she was trying to decide what to tell me. "They're dreams," she then said softly. "It's a sort of dream diary, Robin." She patted the notebook. "My doctor wants me to keep track of all my dreams."

"Really?" I stared at the notebook in surprise. "You write down *all* your dreams? I couldn't ever write mine down; they're crazy. I can't even remember them, anyway."

"That's why I'm writing now," Jen said with a yawn. "The very minute I wake up, before I forget."

"Wow." I kept staring at the notebook. "Are your dreams crazy, like my dreams? Can I see?"

"Well . . ." Her face got that thoughtful look again. Then she shrugged. "Okay, why not? This page isn't too crazy. You can read this."

I plopped down on her bed. Sure enough, there was a date and a paragraph of writing.

I'm in a room, a bedroom I think. I'm trying to open a box—a wooden chest. But I can't get it open. The lid should just lift up; I know that. But I can't get it up. I try and try with all my strength and it just won't budge.

There was another entry below that one. Another date.

The letters again. This time I'm real little. Riding a merry-go-round. A merry-go-round of giant letters. I ride one for a minute, then I get off and wander around, searching all the letters, trying to find the word I want. But I can't.

"Hey, that sounds like—" I stopped. Jen didn't know I had snooped and read her notebook a long time ago. And I hadn't known those were dreams. The same dream almost: giant letters, someone trying to find a word . . .

"Sounds like what?" Jen asked, staring at me intently.

"Sounds like, uh, a crazy dream," I stammered. "But most dreams are crazy anyway. They never make sense." It was all I could think of to say.

"Actually, they do," she said softly. Then in a louder voice, "How about you, Robin? Can you remember any special dreams?"

I wrapped my arms around my knees and thought. "Well, I remember I used to dream a lot about flying." I grinned. "It was really fun, flying all over the place."

She nodded. "Do you know lots of people have flying dreams? They mean something; I don't remember what. Like I said, all dreams have meanings."

"No kidding? Even crazy ones? Is that why you keep a notebook of them?" I pulled her quilt around me. It felt like there were just the two of us, alone in the world, here in Jen's cozy bedroom. Me and my big sister. The special cozy feeling made me brave enough to say softly, "What does your dream mean, Jen?"

Jen was silent. She looked at me, at the notebook, back at me. "Well," she said lightly, "in both dreams, it's like . . . I'm trying to find something. In this second dream, as a little girl, I'm looking for a word . . . a meaning. But . . . I can't . . . find it. . . ." Her voice drifted off.

"Well," I said, to fill the suddenly uneasy silence, "one thing about dreams. They're not real. You always wake up."

"Yeah." Jen gave a short, bitter laugh. "You always wake up. Only you don't, Robin. Some nightmares you don't wake up from." It was her I've-been-around-a-lot-longer-than-you-and-I-know-what-I'm-talking-about voice. But the look on her face wasn't bossy; it was sad, incredibly sad. She opened her mouth as if she were going to say more. We looked at each other. There was this electric tingling feeling for that instant. She was going to tell me something. About "it." The problem. Her problem. The air crackled with the waiting . . . for her to say something . . . for me to ask something.

The moment passed. Jen looked down. She shut the notebook. "Enough about crazy old dreams. It's morning." She threw back the covers. "Let's go fix breakfast." She got out of bed, threw on her robe, and headed for the bathroom.

I watched her go. I leaned back against her headboard, feeling flat, disappointed. The moment had come and gone. We'd almost talked. Something important had almost happened.

Impulsively I grabbed Jen's pen and notebook. At the bottom of the page, below the dream paragraph I wrote the question I should have asked. "What was the little girl in your dream looking for? What's wrong?" I shut the notebook quickly, before I could change my mind and scratch it out. And I left the room.

We had a regular party for breakfast.

"Bacon and eggs and coffee cake! Come and get it!" Jen hollered down the hall. She was wearing Mom's apron over a pretty pink blouse and crisp white pants.

"Hey, I could get spoiled in a hurry with you around,"

Mom teased. She kissed Jen. "You look very nice in that outfit."

"It's my favorite outfit," Jen said cheerily. "I love this pastel pink." She wrapped a piece of coffee cake in a napkin and tossed it to me. "Catch, Robin!"

The coffee cake tasted terrific. Mom knew after one bite that we'd changed the recipe.

"You know," she said to Jen, "you could even leave the coffee cake out completely and just eat cinnamon-sugar filling."

"Not a bad idea." Jen winked at me. "Hey, after breakfast, let me do your hair, okay?"

My hair was long enough for a short ponytail again. But Jen didn't stop with just a ponytail; she took sections of hair and wound them around the rubber band so that I had the most stylish-looking ponytail in town when she was through.

"Thanks, Jen!"

Surprisingly, she reached over and kissed my forehead.

"You're a good kid, Robin," she said softly. "You'll do all right."

I looked at her, puzzled. But she waved me away, smiling. "Have a good day, slaving away while I sit around and watch soap operas. Say hi to Sister Agnes Joseph for me!"

Jen was brave. I thought about how brave she was all the way to school. Here she was, on the outs with Gary, and having to go to a psychiatrist and have treatments and everything.

And she'd fixed breakfast for us. Fixed my hair. Kept on smiling.

She was always trying to be cheerful and giving parties, like my luau party and the shopping party, the pool party and all the other parties for special occasions. "Jen likes to throw parties," Mom told me once. "It cheers her up. Gives her something happy to work on."

I tried hard to pay attention in school. Sister was reading some of our reports. Her words sort of floated above my head.

"Robert has done his report on the holy days, class." She picked up his paper and started reading: "The early popes had trouble getting the pagan people to celebrate the Catholic Holy Days when they first became Christians. These people wanted to keep their own holy days, honoring their pagan gods."

Sister looked up. "That's true, boys and girls. Take Christmas, for example. Some of the pagans had their own midwinter celebrations. They felt that the shortest day of the year, the winter solstice, was holy. So after a while, the Church let them mix some of their customs with the Christian holy days. Like the custom of hanging mistletoe, for example."

Wow. Sister Teresa must have gone to Jen's college. I could just picture Jen sitting on the couch at home last year, saying those very same words. And I'd laughed and told her that Sister Agnes Joseph would excommunicate her for saying that we got Christmas customs from the pagans.

Midwinter festival!

The idea hit like a bolt of lightning. I sat up straighter in my chair. I started doodling like mad in my catechism book, because all of a sudden I felt so excited that I couldn't keep still.

A party!

I could give Jen a party. I could give *her* a good time for a change, the way she'd always done for me.

A midwinter festival party. It was the greatest idea I'd ever had!

I raised my hand. "Sister, what kind of things did the pagans do at their midwinter celebrations?" I asked, trying to sound casual.

Sister looked surprised. "Well, Robin, it's not really important, but of course they had the evergreen branches that they brought into their homes—to keep away devils, I think. Those people were very superstitious."

"Hanging of the greens." I suddenly remembered Jen's words exactly. Because it had sounded like the words of a Christmas carol that day.

I'd get lots of evergreens. Jen loved evergreens. And we'd hang them! And make wreaths out of them. Jen loved making wreaths, too. We'd sing old English carols. And I'd invite Georgie and Lynn. Maybe we could wear pagan clothes, whatever they were.

I wanted to tell Jen all about my idea. Then she could start looking forward to it. I didn't even want to wait till school was over.

I'd go home for lunch and tell her.

I kept thinking about all the details as I walked home. What else had Jen said would be fun to do at a midwinter festival?

Ale! That was it!

There wasn't really time to stop at the grocery store on lunch hour, but I ran in anyway and went over to a teenage guy stocking soups on the shelf.

"Do you sell ale?" I asked breathlessly.

He stared at me. "Do we sell what?"

"Ale."

"Ale?"

"Yeah. *Ale*," I almost yelled. The clerk started to grin.

"Hey, Tony," he yelled to a guy pushing a long broom down the aisle. "We got ale? This kid wants ale."

"Ale?"

"Yeah, ale."

I shook my head. No wonder they just worked in a grocery store. No brains at all.

"I think it's some kind of beer, ain't it?" The one called Tony raised his voice, calling to the butcher three aisles away: "Hey, Wayne, ain't ale some kind of beer?"

"Ale?"

"Yeah, ale."

"Who wants ale?"

I didn't wait to hear the rest. I turned and fled, red faced, back out to the street. Never ever again would I ask for something if I didn't know what it was.

And I'd wasted time in that stupid store. I'd have to run the rest of the way if I wanted to have time for lunch.

My plan was to burst right in and tell Jen all about my great party idea. But when I got home, the TV was on in the living room, with no one watching it, and Jen's door was closed.

"Jen?" I called, softly, in case she was asleep. "Jen?"

No answer. She was taking a nap, then. Sometimes she took medicine that made her drowsy. Well, I could wait a little. If she didn't wake up before it was time to leave, I'd turn the TV up real loud.

I rummaged through the refrigerator and pulled out the tuna fish to make a quick sandwich.

28

I WANT TO STOP THINKING ABOUT THIS. BUT my mind won't stop; it's going full speed now. The memories, frozen for this whole day, are coming in sharp quick bursts—

Like the shot from the bedroom.

Jen's cry, full of pain. Me, jumping up from the table, running down the hall, thinking this is the longest hall in the world. Thinking, God, don't let it be her head. *Please, God,* I just couldn't stand that, if it's her head.

She is lying on the floor of her bedroom, moaning, half-conscious. The pink pastel blouse has a red circle spilling onto it, growing bigger. She still has the gun in her hand.

"I'm sorry, God," she whispers, "but I'm going to do it again." Her hand lifts.

I lunge. For one terrifying split second we both are fighting for that loaded gun.

But she has no strength, she isn't even aware of me trying to take it away. Her fingers relax around the trigger, letting go of the gun. I grab the gun, set it on the bed. It could have gone off when we were struggling, with her finger on the trigger.

I'm shaking so hard I can't think.

I've got to do something. Got to get help.

Jen's still lying there, moaning, gasping.

The phone. All numbers have flown from my brain. Except "O" for Operator.

My voice isn't a voice; it's a sob.

"Ambulance," I finally manage, "I need an ambulance—please—"

The operator knows something's real wrong. She tries to help me. "Your address—can you tell me your address?"

She has to say it three times. I tell her a number. It comes out automatically. Then I think, Is that right?

I run back to Jen; she's slipping in and out of consciousness, moaning one minute, still the next. There's not much blood, just that big red circle in the middle of her pink blouse.

I kneel down by her. "The ambulance is coming, Jen," I whisper.

What else should I do? I have to do something, can't stay still. I run to the front window, checking for the ambulance; I run back to Jen; go over to the phone again.

There's a siren screaming down the street now.

I did give the right address. Because suddenly everyone in the world seems to be pouring into the living room.

First the ambulance people with a stretcher. Then the neighbors, then the police with notebooks and questions.

Then Mom and Dad—who called them? Mom's face is white. She's got her arm around me; she's trying to keep her voice calm, steady.

"Sit down, Robin. Tell us what happened." Over and over. Dad, too.

"Tell us what happened. Talk, Robin. Tell us."

But I just sit there with my shoulders hunched forward, shaking. I don't say much to anyone. Don't even know how many shots. Should cry; can't cry.

Someone has wrapped a blanket around me, tight. It helps.

The day rolled over me like an ice sheet: cold, relentless, numbing. Jen in surgery. Mom and Dad taking turns—one with me, one waiting at the hospital.

"She'll be okay," they said finally. One bullet went in. It didn't touch her heart.

Friends and relatives calling. Aunt Donna and Uncle Robert driving up from San Diego staying late at the house, talking, talking. Me moving around the house like a zombie, getting ready for bed.

I found the purple notebook in my clothes drawer, on top of my pajamas. The dream pages had been ripped out. Instead there was a letter.

Dear Robin,
You wanted to know about the little girl in my dreams. Me, when I was little. Well, she was hurt by someone. A neighbor. A man. It went on a long time. Do you know what kind of hurt

I mean? I mean molested. That's what happened. And that's the word I was looking for in my dreams—in the forest of letters. The word that would tell me the name for what happened to me. Molest.

You won't really understand now. This kind of hurt, what it is, what it does. But you'll understand later, when you're older. I want you to know. So you won't have to search through alphabet dream forests to find the words—the meaning of all this. I love you.

Jen

There was a fierce burning in my throat. The words blurred. Hot tears fell, three or four. No more. The hurt swelled behind my eyes, blocking the rest. I tried so hard to crumple up the notebook that the spiral wires jabbed my palm.

My eyes went to the dark wall where my picture hung. Now at least I knew why the little girl looked so lost, so scared.

Now at last the dark shadow of long ago had a name. Molest.

I think . . . I knew it was something like that. I think something inside me guessed it was that sort of thing.

I flopped backward on my bed, shut my eyes, tried to make sleep come.

Instead there were voices, from the kitchen.

"Look, we don't have all the answers." Dad's voice sounded very far away. "But we had a good talk with the psychiatrist yesterday. I like the man. Sounds like he truly cares about Jen."

Was this my same dad who's always muttering about "that fool headshrinker"?

I heard Uncle Robert's voice, also far away, almost like in a dream. "All this must have happened *years* ago. Wouldn't you think, if it's true about this baby-sitter, Jen would have told *somebody*?"

Silence.

Then Mom's voice. "It seems he threatened Jen. That's what the psychiatrist says, anyway."

"What—"

"He supposedly told Jen . . . that he'd come back from the dead and get her if she told what happened."

"Dear God."

"That's where Lent fits in. Why Lent is her worst time. Lent and Easter. The idea of someone rising from the dead terrified her as a child. . . ." Now Mom was crying.

Then I heard Aunt Donna. "I just can't believe it. I'm hearing it and I . . . can't believe it."

"That's the problem. Believing. Accepting." It was hard to understand Mom's voice, now so full of crying. "But, after yesterday . . . we've *got* to. We must become involved in these sessions with her psychiatrist. We've *got* to be."

"That poor girl." Aunt Donna's voice broke. "That poor girl."

That poor girl. Poor little girl. My eyes went again to

the dark wall where my picture hung, then to the crumpled purple notebook under my hand.

"If she'd only *told* someone—even *one* person." It was Uncle Robert again.

I gripped the notebook hard. She told *me.* She did. Right here in this notebook. But only because she thought . . . she tried to . . .

No! I threw the notebook down on the floor.

I'd changed my mind. I didn't want to go to sleep. I wanted to wake up. I wanted this to all be a dream, and I wanted to wake up from it!

But Jen said there are some nightmares you don't wake up from.

Part 5

Four Days
Before Christmas—1960

29

SO. MY THOUGHTS HAVE COME FULL CIRCLE—
like this Hula Hoop I am clutching in my hand on my way
to the hospital.

I'm almost at the edge of the park. I don't remember
crossing the whole park. I don't remember if I took the
paths or tromped across the grass. I don't remember seeing
the swings and slides.

While my feet were crossing this park, my mind was on
a different trip, a long, painful one.

What did Sister call those long, painful trips to sacred
places? Pilgrimages. That's it.

So I've been a pilgrim, I guess. A time pilgrim, traveling
to the sacred places of my past, trying to make sense of it
all. And I don't need to crawl up a mountain or go barefoot,
or to add any more penance and pain. There's enough pain
already.

I've reached the edge of the park. Wilson Street is decorated for Christmas. There are lights twinkling up and
down the whole street. It's like staring at another world. I
stand here blinking. How could I have forgotten about
Christmas?

There are two ways I can take now to get to the hospital. I can cross Wilson and walk up that busy, brightly lit street, or I can keep to this side of the street, where the park ends and the city cemetery begins.

I'll take the brightly lit side. I'm not in the mood for a cemetery right now. Even if I look strange carrying a Hula Hoop, I can't just leave it here, now that I've lugged it this far.

Some Salvation Army people are on the opposite corner, ringing bells; some women and kids are hurrying down the sidewalk, carrying packages in their arms. A real Christmas scene. Maybe someone will think I bought this Hula Hoop for a Christmas present. Except it's so dirty. . . .

I start to cross the street—and stop. I pull back.

That's Georgie, across the road, walking with some boy, holding hands, having a great old time. I know Georgie's walk. I know that outfit.

Is school out already? I do not want to meet Georgie right now. Not after what's happened. She knows about it, of course. Everybody must know. It was in the newspaper and everything.

Georgie wouldn't know what to say. She'd be embarrassed, especially with a boy there. I'd feel like a jerk. Her holding hands with a boy, and me holding hands with a Hula Hoop. I guess I'd rather face the tombstones than Georgie right now.

Someone has decorated the cemetery for Christmas. Every single tombstone has a wreath with a red bow set up against it. There's actually a kind of peaceful feeling here at the edge of the cemetery. It's a peaceful time of day, sunset. My favorite. The sun is hanging at the lowest edge of the sky.

Have I been walking so long? But then, the sun sets early this time of year. Sister was just talking about that. The winter solstice. The shortest day of the year. Four days before Christmas, nowadays—December twenty-first.

That's today. *This* is the day the pagans had their parties . . . brought evergreens into their houses to try to make the sun go higher in the sky.

I would have had a party, Jen. I *would* have . . .

Jen likes wreaths so much. I wish I had the nerve to grab one of those gravestone wreaths; just yank it right off and bring it with me to the hospital.

That would probably be a mortal sin—robbing the dead.

Looking at all those wreaths on all those gravestones, I think for the first time: Those were people once. They walked around, ate, worked, had families and friends.

Did any of them die from a gunshot wound?

Right this minute I'm glad that Jen is in the hospital. Because if she weren't there, she'd be . . . here.

That's what dead means. I never really thought about the word *dead* before.

There's a lot of noise coming from the corner. Laughing, yelling, talking. It doesn't seem respectful, here with all these tombstones.

It's a family making the racket. I'm walking in their direction. I can see them better now; they're laughing because they're trying to carry a huge Christmas tree and the kids keep dropping it. They're probably breaking branches off it, too.

There's a Christmas-tree lot across the street, crowded in between two gas stations. And there are other people carrying out trees. Watching them, I think about the argument Jen and Mom have every year: real trees versus fake trees.

"Nothing fake can make a room smell like Christmas," Jen always says stubbornly.

I walk faster. There are broken branches on the sidewalk and on the grass. Lots of branches, from the trees everyone's been carrying all week. I start picking up branches. If Jen is . . . conscious . . . then she would like her hospital room to smell like Christmas.

It's not as good as a wreath, though. If only I had one of those wire wreath frames like Jen uses, or anything round to wrap the branches around.

Round.

I stare at my Hula Hoop, which is looped over my right arm. It'd make one of the biggest wreaths ever! I scramble around, grabbing up branches from the grass, the sidewalk. A whole armful. That should be enough.

It's hard to attach branches to plastic. I wind them around and they snap back off. I twist them and they break.

The smallest ones are the most pliable. I can even tie some of them in knots around the Hula Hoop. And once those are in place, I can attach new branches to them, looping, twisting, tying. I can use skinny branches to help tie on big branches, and more big branches, all the way around the big yellow circle of the Hula Hoop.

Done. The world's skinniest wreath. It looks more like a giant bracelet than a wreath.

It *needs* something. A red bow would help.

I don't have the guts to steal a whole wreath from the dead, but I do have the guts to swipe just a single red bow. That's not so bad. Not if it's for a gift—for Jen. And the wreath over by the tall, thin gravestone even has a loose bow. Just one little yank and it's off, wire and all.

I march off holding my Hula Hoop wreath—for the last three blocks of my pilgrimage to the hospital.

30

"JENNIFER McCORD?" THE RECEPTIONIST looks up at me. "She's in room three forty-five. But there's restricted visiting. Family only."

"I'm family." I start for the elevator.

"Wait, miss, how old are you?" She's half-risen, calling after me.

They'll never let a thirteen-year-old in. "Sixteen," I lie, and hurry through the lobby. There's an elevator waiting to rescue me, doors wide open. It takes me up and delivers me to the third floor. The doors open. I step out and stand there, blinking.

Did the elevator goof and take me back to St. Ignatius School? There's Father Smith, the pastor, and—oh, no—there are Sister Agnes Joseph *and* Sister Teresa. And Dad.

What's going on? Did they come to see why I never made it back to school after lunch yesterday?

Restricted visiting. Sure. Nuns and priests always get special privileges.

"Robin!" Dad takes great long strides down the hall to me. "How in the world did you get here? Who brought you?" Everyone is staring at me and my Hula Hoop.

"I . . . walked. I wanted to see Jen."

"Walked! Good Lord!" he cries. "The house is over two miles away! Robin, we didn't mean to leave you at home for so long. But Jen's doctor was here, and then the psychiatrist, and Father Smith and the Sisters . . ."

Father Smith comes over beside me. "Your sister's going to be fine, Robin." He has a calm, soothing voice. "That's what the doctor said just now. She'll pull through just fine." He looks straight at me. "Jen can thank *you* for that, Robin."

I don't want to stand here in the hall. I want to go into that room and see Jen. That's what I came on my long pilgrimage for. I nod at Father politely. I walk over and open Jen's closed door. Number three forty-five. I carry my Hula Hoop in. Mom's by the bed. She gets up in surprise when she sees me.

"Robin!"

And there's Jen. Pale. Her hair like tangled silk all over the pillow. She has an ugly hospital gown on. Her eyes are closed. I just stand there looking. My heart's pounding. I lift up my Hula Hoop wreath and set it on her little table, propped against the wall. Soon it will fill this room with Christmas and cover up that medicine smell.

This is Midwinter Day, after all. I like the idea those pagans had, bringing greens inside, to stand for life, for hope, when the sun is at its lowest point in the sky . . . to pray that it will rise again.

Everyone is standing just inside the doorway.

"Robin." Mom comes behind me and puts both hands on

my shoulders. A firm, caring grip. "You see. She's sleeping now. She'll be okay."

"Robin." It's Sister Agnes Joseph. I never would have believed she could speak so softly and gently. "Robin, you found your sister when you went home for lunch?"

"Yes, Sister."

"Robin." She pauses. "Have you ever gone home for lunch before?"

"No, Sister."

Sister's voice drops even more. She sounds hoarse. "Then why yesterday . . . ?"

I can't tell Sister Agnes Joseph that I was planning a pagan party for Jen.

"I don't know, Sister. I just . . . did."

Both Sisters are staring at me with very intense looks on their faces. The room is totally silent.

"And this is the girl who said there are no more miracles," Sister Teresa murmurs very softly.

"You love your sister very much, don't you, Robin?"

There comes a moment when everything is too much. I can feel the wave starting to rise inside me, churning up from my stomach, swelling, gathering force, power . . .

Bursting, exploding, flooding everywhere: my nose, my eyes, my mouth, every part of me shaking with sobs that come from so deep inside me that it feels like I'm throwing up instead of crying. On and on and on . . . like I will never stop until my insides are gone.

"It's okay. Cry it out. Let it out."

"She needs to do this. She's got to get it out. . . ."

I can't make sense of anything. Arms are around me; I'm burying my face in something warm and black.

Oh my God, it's Sister Agnes Joseph. I am doing the unthinkable, the unforgivable. I am crying all over Sister Agnes Joseph. Even extreme circumstances, even a near death in the family, don't excuse such behavior. I hope no one from St. Ignatius School is anywhere near this hospital.

Still, it's a long time before I can pull away, shuddering, hiccuping.

I'm being such a baby. I can't stand to have them all see me like this. I want to shut the door, shut them all out, not have to face anybody, ever again.

I look around desperately for an escape. The room's crowded. Nowhere to go. People in the doorway, Dad by the bed. Mom here beside me, her arm around my shoulder.

And . . . someone has hung my wreath. Balanced it right over a picture hanging on the wall.

Hanging of the greens. December twenty-first. No ale. Not exactly what I planned. This is no party.

But the sun is so low now it's shining straight in through the window, sending a strange, pale light over us. Tiny dust pieces are whirling around in that light. Sunbeams, Mom used to call them. Clap your hands, Robin. Catch the sunbeams.

Hey, Jen, remember when I was little, how I used to say that you got the best room, because it was bigger? Well, Jen, it's a good thing I didn't move to your room after you moved out. One important thing about *my* room: it's close to the kitchen. I heard lots of things, Jen. I heard Mom say she believed those things you told her. And Dad—I heard *him* say that he liked your doctor. Jen, that's *something*. Did you know he always used to call your doctor a damn headshrinker?

Do you hear that sound in the doorway, Jen? *Clack, clack, swish?* Yep, all of us who go to Catholic school know that sound: the old rosary bead *clack-clack*. One of the Sisters must be praying. Sometimes they're not so bad. They're rooting for you, Jen.

I'm glad you wrote me that letter in the purple notebook. Maybe when you get home we could talk . . . maybe.

And I could make a sign. It could say: GET WELL, JEN or WELCOME HOME or something like that.

The late sunlight is washing over the whole room, making everything seem like a dream, unreal, glowing.

Hey, Jen, there was this kid named Robin. She was so childish. She'd have probably jumped up and down yelling, "Halo, halo, miracle," about this weird light. She thought she could catch a miracle the way you catch a sunbeam.

Well, that's a crazy word—miracle. I don't really know what it's made of.

One thing I *do* know, Jen. You're going to wake up from this nightmare. The doctor said so. You'll get better.

There's something you're going to like, when you wake up—

Jen, this room is really starting to smell like evergreens.

If You Need Help

JEN'S STORY IS THE STORY OF A SECRET KEPT too long. Today the issue of sexual abuse is dealt with more openly. Counselors urge children to talk to a trusted adult; if that adult does nothing, to tell another trusted adult, and to keep telling until someone gets help.

For those who don't want to talk to someone they know, there is a National Child Abuse Hotline number to call:

1-800-422-4453

(1-800-4-A-CHILD)

Such secrets can and must be told.